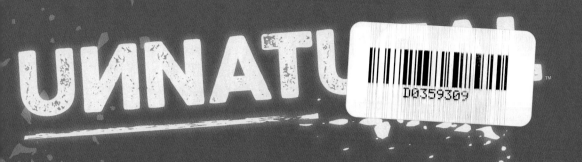

UNNATURAL

VOLUME TWO · THE HUNT

writer, artist and colorist
MIRKA ANDOLFO

colors assistant
GIANLUCA PAPI
(ARANCIA STUDIO)

lettering and production
FABIO AMELIA
(ARANCIA STUDIO)

translation from italian
ARANCIA STUDIO

cover artist
MIRKA ANDOLFO

editors
DIEGO MALARA
MARCO RICOMPENSA

design
ALESSANDRO GUCCIARDO
FABIO AMELIA

CHAPTER FIVE

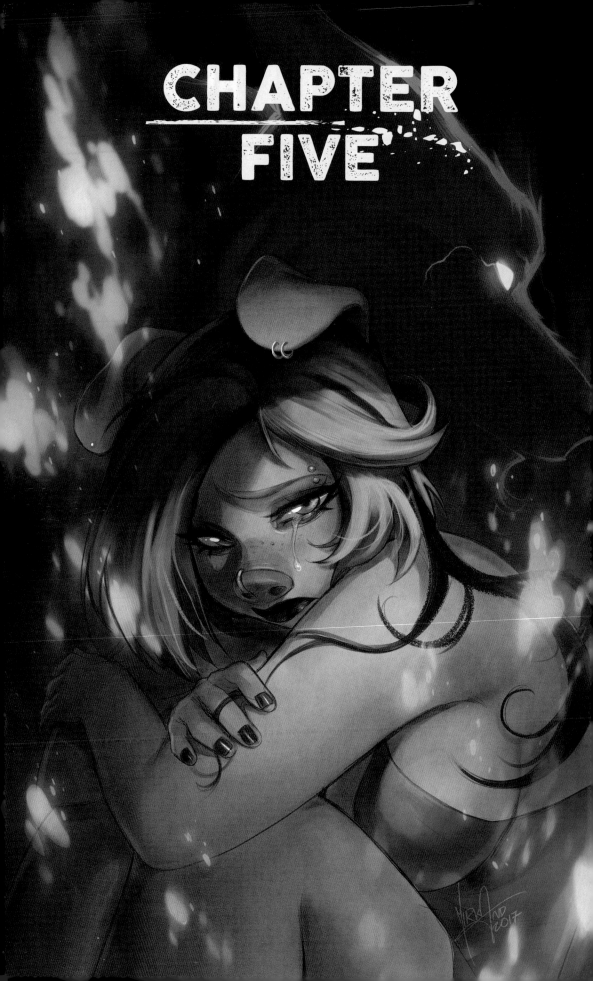

MIRKA ANDOLFO'S

UNNATURAL™

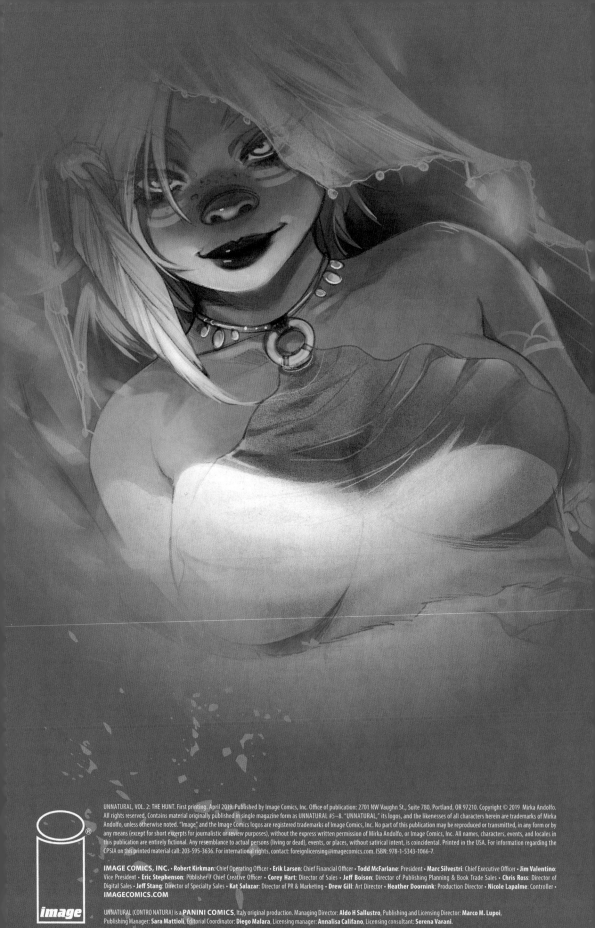

UNNATURAL, VOL. 2: THE HUNT. First printing. April 2019. Published by Image Comics, Inc. Office of publication: 2701 NW Vaughn St., Suite 780, Portland, OR 97210. Copyright © 2019 Mirka Andolfo. All rights reserved. Contains material originally published in single magazine form as UNNATURAL #5–8. "UNNATURAL," its logos, and the likenesses of all characters herein are trademarks of Mirka Andolfo, unless otherwise noted. "Image" and the Image Comics logos are registered trademarks of Image Comics, Inc. No part of this publication may be reproduced or transmitted, in any form or by any means (except for short excerpts for journalistic or review purposes), without the express written permission of Mirka Andolfo, or Image Comics, Inc. All names, characters, events, and locales in this publication are entirely fictional. Any resemblance to actual persons (living or dead), events, or places, without satirical intent, is coincidental. Printed in the USA. For information regarding the CPSIA on this printed material call: 203-595-3636. For international rights, contact: foreignlicensing@imagecomics.com. ISBN: 978-1-5343-1066-7.

IMAGE COMICS, INC. • **Robert Kirkman**: Chief Operating Officer • **Erik Larsen**: Chief Financial Officer • **Todd McFarlane**: President • **Marc Silvestri**: Chief Executive Officer • **Jim Valentino**: Vice President • **Eric Stephenson**: Publisher / Chief Creative Officer • **Corey Hart**: Director of Sales • **Jeff Boison**: Director of Publishing Planning & Book Trade Sales • **Chris Ross**: Director of Digital Sales • **Jeff Stang**: Director of Specialty Sales • **Kat Salazar**: Director of PR & Marketing • **Drew Gill**: Art Director • **Heather Doornink**: Production Director • **Nicole Lapalme**: Controller • IMAGECOMICS.COM

UNNATURAL (CONTRO NATURA) is a **PANINI COMICS**, Italy original production. Managing Director: **Aldo H Sallustro**, Publishing and Licensing Director: **Marco M. Lupoi**, Publishing Manager: **Sara Mattioli**, Editorial Coordinator: **Diego Malara**, Licensing manager: **Annalisa Califano**, Licensing consultant: **Serena Varani**.

New Roark.
BRROM
PEEE
PEEE
FIII
PEEE
CLIC
GOOD MORNING. LICENSE AND REGISTRATION, PLEASE...

WHAT SEEMS TO BE THE PROBLEM, OFFICER?
JUST A ROUTINE CHECK, MA'AM.
OKAY, JUST A SECOND...
COME ON! WHERE DID I PUT IT? NOT HERE...NOT HERE...
HOW CAN I HAVE THIS MUCH JUNK IN MY BAG?
SHE SEEMS NERVOUS.
YOU THINK?
HERE IT IS!
THANK YOU. WOULD YOU MIND IF WE CHECKED YOUR LOAD?
WHAT? I MEAN, ACTUALLY I'M KIND OF IN A HURRY...
SO ARE WE, THIS WON'T TAKE LONG.
PROVIDED EVERYTHING CHECKS OUT, THIS SHOULD BE QUICK.
JUST NEED TO FIND THE RIGHT KEY...
CLACK
THERE YOU GO, OFFICERS... PRETTY WILD LOAD, HUH?

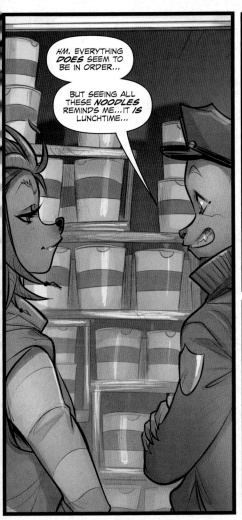

HM. EVERYTHING *DOES* SEEM TO BE IN ORDER...

BUT SEEING ALL THESE *NOODLES* REMINDS ME...IT *IS* LUNCHTIME...

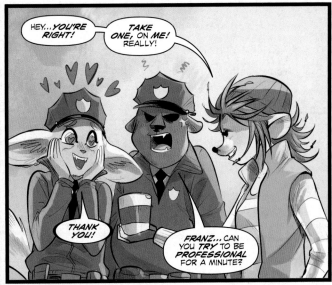

HEY...*YOU'RE RIGHT!*

TAKE *ONE,* ON *ME!* REALLY!

THANK *YOU!*

*FRANZ...*CAN YOU *TRY* TO BE *PROFESSIONAL* FOR A MINUTE?

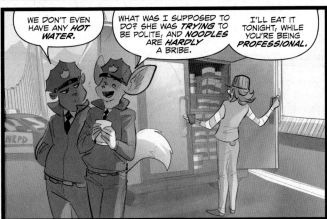

WE DON'T EVEN HAVE ANY *HOT WATER.*

WHAT WAS I SUPPOSED TO DO? SHE WAS *TRYING* TO BE POLITE, AND *NOODLES* ARE *HARDLY* A BRIBE.

I'LL EAT IT TONIGHT, WHILE YOU'RE BEING *PROFESSIONAL.*

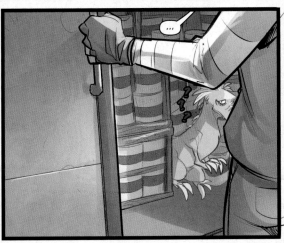

...

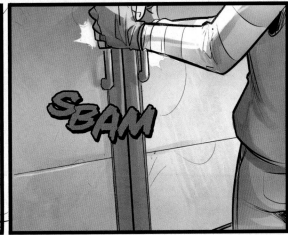

SBAM

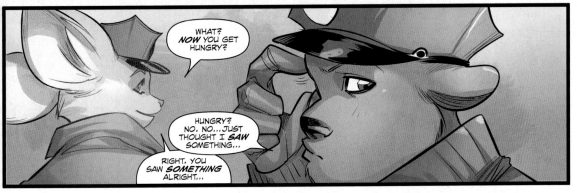

WHAT? *NOW* YOU GET HUNGRY?

HUNGRY? NO. NO...JUST THOUGHT I *SAW* SOMETHING...

RIGHT. YOU SAW *SOMETHING* ALRIGHT...

HER ASS. SOME OFFICER YOU ARE...
SHUT UP, FRANZ! DON'T BE AN IDIOT.
...CAN YOU GO ANY FASTER?
NOT WITH YOU BUSTING MY BALLS, I CAN'T.
THERE'S STILL A WAYS TO GO.
EASY FOR YOU TO SAY, YOU'RE NOT HIDING BACK HERE!
THIS PLACE STINKS!
AND AS FOR YOU, LESLIE BLAIR... YOU NEED TO KEEP THAT BEAST IN CHECK!
AHH!
CRUNCH

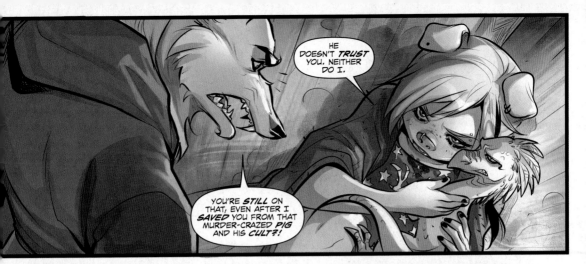

HE DOESN'T *TRUST* YOU. NEITHER DO I.

YOU'RE *STILL* ON THAT, EVEN AFTER I *SAVED* YOU FROM THAT MURDER-CRAZED *PIG* AND HIS *CULT*?!

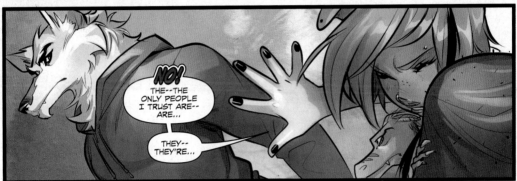

NO! THE--THE ONLY PEOPLE I TRUST ARE-- ARE...

THEY-- THEY'RE...

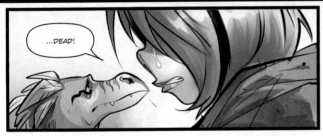

...DEAD!

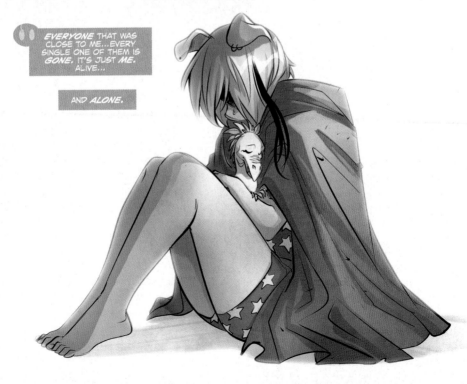

EVERYONE THAT WAS CLOSE TO ME...EVERY SINGLE ONE OF THEM IS *GONE.* IT'S JUST *ME.* ALIVE...

AND *ALONE.*

OH, BUT LESLIE...DON'T CRY. YOU'RE NOT ALONE.
I'M HERE WITH YOU!
I WILL ALWAYS BE HERE TO WATCH OVER YOU, MY BRIDE...
...WHETHER YOU LIKE IT OR NOT!
NO! GO AWAY!
?

AAAARGH!
!
SBRAAANGH
NO, NO! SOMEONE HELP!
YOU NEED TO CALM DOWN, LESLIE.
SOMEONE WILL HEAR US!
TRISH! DEREK! ANYONE!
HELP ME!
SSSH...
TRISH, DEREK...
TRISH...

DEREK... THE POOR BOY! HE WAS ONE OF MY BEST WAITERS, COMPLETELY DEDICATED TO "GOTH LOL," MY BEAUTIFUL RESTAURANT THAT OPENED ITS ARMS TO HIM... THAT HE WAS PROUD TO WORK IN!
WHAT WAS THAT? THE SECOND VICTIM? I--I DIDN'T KNOW HER QUITE AS WELL, BUT... SHE WAS A GREAT "GOTH LOL" CUSTOMER... SHE CALLED US "THE BEST DINER IN TOWN"!
ANIMAL NEWS
THE EMPLOYER
ME? AMAZED? NO. NOT AT ALL...
I ALWAYS KNEW SOMETHING WAS UP WITH THAT LESLIE BLAIR... NO SURPRISE SHE'S ONE OF THOSE CROSS-SPECIES PERVERTS!
I TOLD TRISH SHE WAS A WEIRDO... PROBABLY GROOMING HER TOO! THOSE PEOPLE WILL DO ANYTHING!
ANIMAL NEWS
A FRIEND OF THE VICTIM
I KNEW LESLIE WAS TOO ATTACHED TO TRISH...
OUR DAUGHTER WASN'T LIKE THAT... BUT LESLIE WOULDN'T ACCEPT THAT; WANTED MORE THAN FRIENDSHIP...
ANIMAL NEWS
THE PARENTS OF THE VICTIM
THAT SHAMELESS PIG JUST COULDN'T TAKE THAT MY SWEET BABY WAS NORMAL! NOT SOME FILTHY...
ANIMAL NEWS
THE PARENTS OF THE VICTIM
...UNNATURAL PIG...
ANIMAL NEWS
THE PARENTS OF THE VICTIM
...LIKE HER!
ANIMAL NEWS
THE PARENTS OF THE VICTIM
SO, VIEWERS... WAS THIS FORBIDDEN ATTRACTION... OR FATAL ATTRACTION?
WAS LESLIE BLAIR'S INFATUATION WITH TRISH FRIHA THE CAUSE OF A MURDEROUS RAGE THAT TOOK NOT JUST FRIHA'S LIFE, BUT THAT OF THEIR TRUSTED FRIEND DEREK?
FOR NOW, IT'S AN OPEN QUESTION, SINCE BLAIR REMAINS AT LARGE! IF YOU HAVE ANY INFORMATION AS TO HER WHEREABOUTS, PLEASE CONTACT THE AUTHORITIES IMMEDIATELY.
BUT BE WARNED, LESLIE BLAIR IS CONSIDERED ARMED...

...AND EXTREMELY DANGEROUS.
HEY...GOOD MORNING.
ARE YOU FEELING RESTED? I COULD PLAY SOME MORE...
DEPENDS...
CAN I TAKE OFF THIS STUPID WIG?
OR YOU AT LEAST HAVE TO LET ME IN ON THE JOKE.
WHAT THE FUCK DO YOU THINK YOU'RE DOING?
I'M--I'M SORRY! I DIDN'T MEAN-- I...
GET THE FUCK OUT OF HERE! NOW!
TUMP
ASSHOLE!
FUCKING PSYCHO...
PRIVA
THAT'S HOW YOU DEAL WITH WOMEN, "JONES"?
YOU DIDN'T SEEM TO MIND VIOLENCE WHEN I WAS KILLING THAT LITTLE MOUSE THAT KNEW TOO MUCH.
AND TRUST ME, WHEN IT COMES TO VIOLENCE... I GO BOTH WAYS.

HOW ARE YOU NOT *EMBARRASSED* TO LEAVE THE HOUSE IN THAT *CHEAP HALLOWEEN OUTFIT?*

MIND YOURSELF, FOOL! THESE ARE *SACRED* GARMENTS... THEY *IMBUE* ME WITH *GREAT POWER!*

THAT'S RIGHT. YOUR *FAMOUS* POWERS...WHICH *STILL* COULDN'T STOP *EVERYTHING* FROM GOING WRONG WITH *BLAIR.*

EVEN IF YOU *GLANCE* AT EVERYTHING...

ENOUGH OF YOUR *DISRESPECT!*

I'M JUST *STATING THE FACTS,* "MASTER."

BLAIR GOT AWAY. THAT MEANS THERE ARE PEOPLE *ALIVE* THAT KNOW ABOUT OUR PLAN...AND ARE *BEYOND* OUR CONTROL.

BECAUSE OF *YOUR* FAILURES!

THE ONLY ONES WHO CAN KNOW ABOUT THE *PLAN...* ARE THOSE *WE* ALLOW.

THOSE WE DO *NOT...* MUST NOT BE ALLOWED TO *LIVE.* WE MUST MAKE *GOOD* ON THAT...

"...AND FIND THAT BLUE-HAIRED PIG."
?
...WHERE AM I?
I'M SICK OF WAKING UP SOMEWHERE DIFFERENT FROM WHERE I FELL ASLEEP...
!
IN CLOTHES THAT DON'T FIT.
PURRP
PURRP
PIF! ARE YOU OKAY? DID THEY HURT YOU? MY MEMORIES DON'T MAKE SENSE. NONE OF THIS DOES...
I NEED TO KNOW WHERE I AM.
HELLO?!
IS ANYONE THERE?

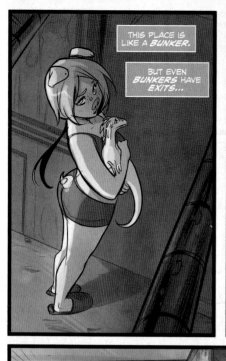

THIS PLACE IS LIKE A *BUNKER.*

BUT EVEN *BUNKERS* HAVE *EXITS...*

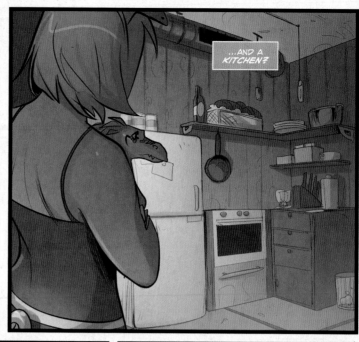

...AND A *KITCHEN?*

WIII

GRO0O0OOO

FOOD! THANK GOD!

FEELS LIKE I HAVEN'T EATEN IN *AGES.*

LEFTOVERS NEVER TASTED SO GOOD!

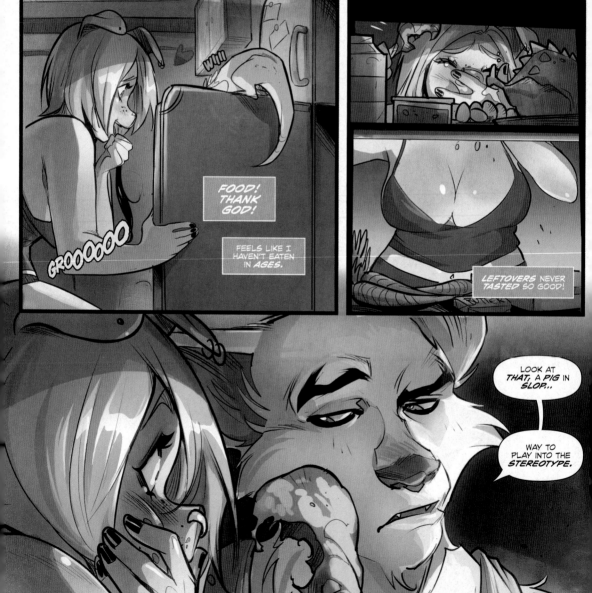

LOOK AT *THAT,* A *PIG* IN *SLOP...*

WAY TO PLAY INTO THE *STEREOTYPE.*

SPLATH
YOU AGAIN?
WHAT KIND OF A THANK YOU IS THAT?
AND THE NAME'S "KHAL," BY THE WAY. NOT "YOU."
THANK YOU, "KHAL." YOU WANT TO TELL ME WHAT THE HELL IS GOING ON?
CAROL IS ON HER WAY TO TELL YOU EVERYTHING. UNTIL THEN, JUST KNOW THAT RIGHT NOW? THIS IS THE SAFEST PLACE FOR YOU.
I'LL DECIDE WHERE I'M SAFEST, IF YOU DON'T MIND...
?
SO, STEP THE HELL BACK! TOUCH ME AGAIN AND YOU'RE WOLF SASHIMI!
HA. SO OUR LITTLE PIG IS A LITTLE BRAVE.
LET ME SHOW YOU SOMETHING...
ARE-- ARE YOU CRAZY?!
CRASH

SEE? NOT SO BAD... YOU WERE SAYING SOMETHING ABOUT STABBING ME?
T-THE... COLOR OF YOUR... BLOOD...
THE COLOR OF MY LEGACY.
YOU SHOULD UNDERSTAND BETTER THAN ANYONE.
ME?! WHY ME?
HERE. PRICK YOUR FINGER...
AND CHECK FOR YOURSELF.
WHAT THE HELL?! MY BLOOD...
IT'S BLUE?!
CROWDED KITCHEN TODAY, EH, KHAL?
CAREFUL, LESLIE...
IT'S DANGEROUS TO PLAY WITH KNIVES LIKE THAT.
SAYA!

YOU WORRIED ABOUT THE PIG HURTING HERSELF? YOU CAN TAKE OVER BABYSITTING. I'VE GOT WORK TO DO...
MPHF! FINE. COME ON, LESLIE. I'LL TAKE YOU TO CAROL...
NOW THAT WE'RE ALONE...A BIT OF ADVICE? TAKE IT EASY ON KHAL, OKAY?
WHAT? I'M THE ONE THAT HAS TO GO EASY?
I'M SUPPOSED TO BELIEVE HE'S SENSITIVE? HE SHATTERED A KNIFE IN HIS BARE PAW! HE'S THE ONE THAT NEEDS TO BE GENTLE WITH ME!
LISTEN, PIG PRINCESS... YOU SHOULD KISS THE GROUND WHEN KHAL WALKS BY, YOU HEAR ME?
YOU THINK YOU'VE BEEN THROUGH A LOT? THINK YOU'VE LOST SO MUCH?
YOU THINK THAT MAKES YOU SPECIAL? WELL...
...IF THAT'S SO, THEN KHAL'S BEEN SPECIAL SINCE THE DAY HE WAS BORN.

"WHAT DO YOU KNOW ABOUT TIJOUX?"
"...NOTHING, BUT THE NAME DOES SOUND FAMILIAR."
"IT'S A PLACE. AND IT'S WHERE ALL YOUR TROUBLES STARTED.
"IT'S NOT LIKE HERE... PEOPLE ARE FREE IN TIJOUX.
"THERE, KHAL WAS BORN INTO A LOVING FAMILY.
"BUT BECAUSE OF HIS FAMILY'S BLOOD, THEY WERE ANYTHING BUT LOVED.
"THEY WERE CALLED INFECTED, WHISPERED TO BE THE MORTAL OFFSPRING OF A SUPREME EVIL...
"KHAL LOOKED JUST LIKE... SOMETHING... FROM THE PAST. SOMEONE ANCIENT, AND TREMENDOUSLY DEADLY."
"...THE WOLF FROM MY DREAMS?"
"THAT'S RIGHT."

HE'S CALLED THE ALBINO.
BY NOW YOU KNOW THAT HE'S NOT AN ORDINARY WOLF.
HE'S A MONSTER. I KNOW THAT.
...AND HE DID SOMETHING TO ME, A LONG TIME AGO.
HE DID SOMETHING TO A LOT OF PEOPLE.
KHAL PAID THE PRICE FOR THE ALBINO'S ACTIONS, JUST BECAUSE OF HOW HE LOOKED.
"WHAT'S WORSE IS THAT HIS FACE ISN'T THE ONLY WAY KHAL RESEMBLES THE ALBINO."
UH?
"HIS STRENGTH IS SUPERNATURAL.
"HIS CLAWS ARE SHARP AS DIAMONDS."

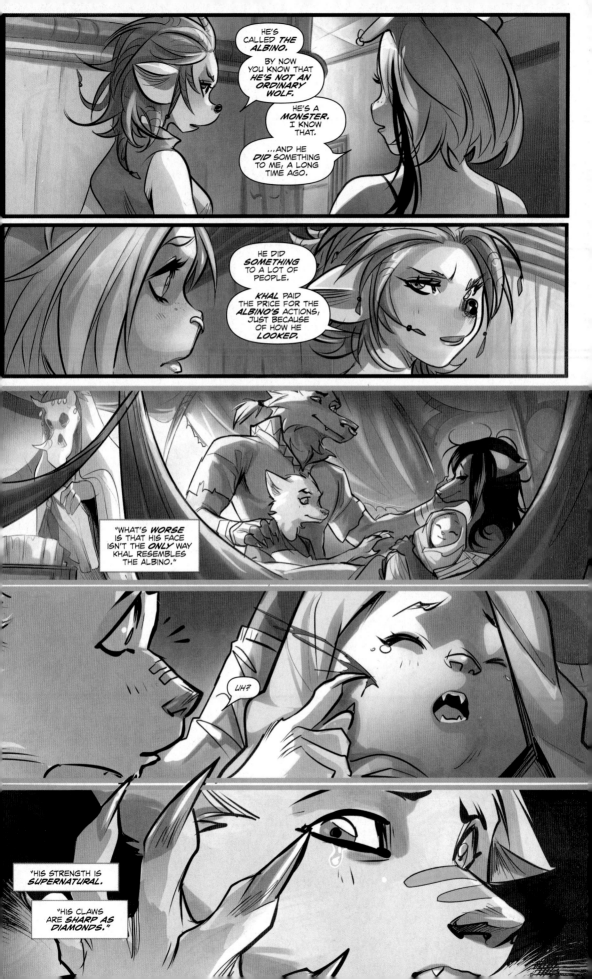

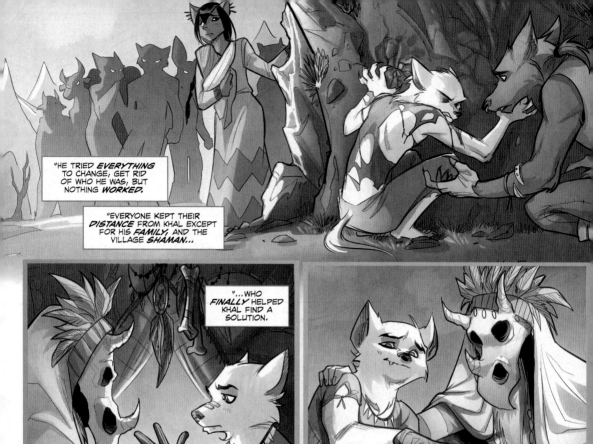

"HE TRIED *EVERYTHING* TO CHANGE, GET RID OF WHO HE WAS, BUT NOTHING *WORKED*.

"EVERYONE KEPT THEIR *DISTANCE* FROM KHAL EXCEPT FOR HIS *FAMILY*, AND THE VILLAGE *SHAMAN*...

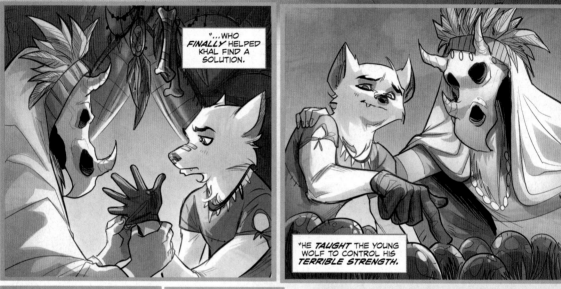

"...WHO *FINALLY* HELPED KHAL FIND A SOLUTION.

"HE *TAUGHT* THE YOUNG WOLF TO CONTROL HIS *TERRIBLE STRENGTH*.

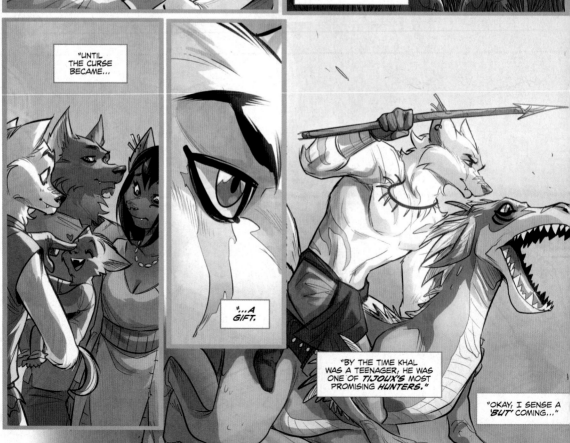

"UNTIL THE CURSE BECAME...

"...A *GIFT*.

"BY THE TIME KHAL WAS A TEENAGER, HE WAS ONE OF *TIJOUX'S* MOST PROMISING *HUNTERS*."

"OKAY, I SENSE A *'BUT'* COMING..."

"YOU DON'T KNOW HOW RIGHT YOU ARE. BECAUSE DESPITE HIS PROGRESS, THE TOWN NEVER STOPPED FEARING KHAL.
"ONE DAY, THERE WAS A DEATH IN TOWN. I DON'T KNOW WHO... KHAL HAS NEVER TOLD ME.
"IT DIDN'T TAKE LONG FOR KHAL, THE TOWN'S OUTCAST, TO BE ACCUSED.
"HE WAS INNOCENT. HIS PARENTS TRIED TO KEEP KHAL SAFE...
"BUT THEY DIED TO SATE THE VENGEFUL TOWN'S THIRST FOR VIOLENCE.
"KHAL WAS IMPRISONED, DRUGGED SO HE COULDN'T ESCAPE. THE TOWN PLANNED TO MAKE HIM A SACRIFICE TO THEIR ANCIENT SPIRITS. HIM...
"...AND HIS YOUNGER SISTER."

THAT STORY... THAT'S HORRIBLE, SAYA.
I KNOW. AND NOW... SO DO YOU.
TOC TOC
COME IN!
"LUCKILY, THANKS TO THE SHAMAN...
"SHE ARRIVED TO SAVE THEM BEFORE THE SACRIFICE.
"KHAL, ME...EVEN YOU... WE ALL OWE A LOT..."
...TO CAROL.
HELLO, LESLIE...
WE FINALLY MEET!

CHAPTER SIX

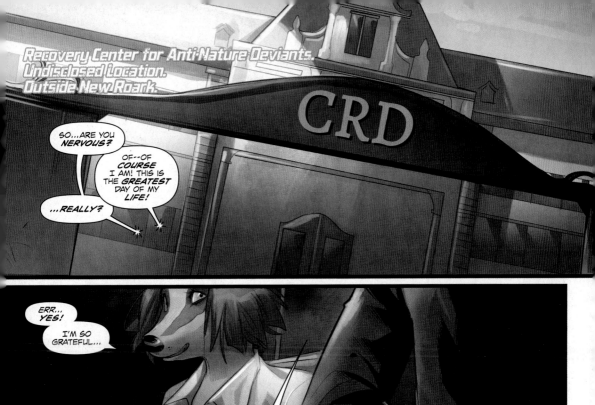

SO...ARE YOU *NERVOUS?*

OF--OF *COURSE* I AM! THIS IS THE *GREATEST* DAY OF MY *LIFE!*

...*REALLY?*

ERR... *YES!*

I'M SO *GRATEFUL...*

THAT'S *FUNNY.* IT *REALLY* IS. IT WASN'T A *MONTH* AGO YOU WERE CALLING ME A *PIECE OF SHIT.*

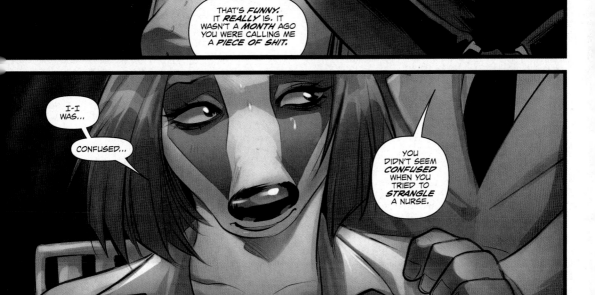

I-I WAS...

CONFUSED...

YOU DIDN'T SEEM *CONFUSED* WHEN YOU TRIED TO *STRANGLE* A NURSE.

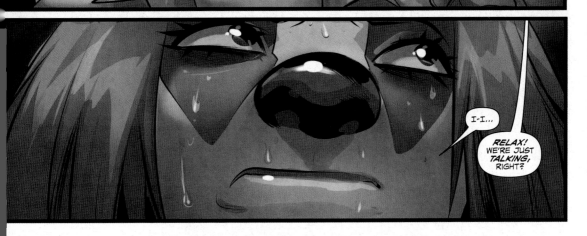

I-I...

RELAX! WE'RE JUST *TALKING,* RIGHT?

IS IT OR IS IT NOT THE GREATEST DAY OF YOUR LIFE?
THOSE SIX MONTHS OF THERAPY ARE NOTHING COMPARED TO THE LIFETIME OF PROMISE AHEAD!
A NATURAL LIFE...A LIFE OF NORMALCY!
MAYBE YOU'RE JUST AFRAID... BECAUSE YOU KNOW YOU'RE A BAD APPLE.
W-WHAT...?
OH...I THINK YOU TOOK MY MEANING.
PEOPLE LIKE YOU NEVER TRULY CHANGE. NEVER.
ALL THIS, EVERYTHING HERE...IT'S NOTHING BUT A SHOW.
IF I ONLY COULD, I'D KILL YOU ALL!
DEET

DOCTOR... THE ELECTROSHOCK CHIP HAS BEEN SUCCESSFULLY EXTRACTED.
TOO BAD WE DIDN'T LOSE HER IN THE PROCESS...
I PROMISED THIS WOULDN'T HURT, NOT MUCH MORE THAN A SHOT, AT LEAST. AS YOU'VE SEEN...
I LIED.
MY--MY FOREHEAD... WHY IS IT BURNING?
ENJOY IT... IT'S ONLY THE BEGINNING.
MY SKIN... IS--IS IT...
A TATTOO.
AN INEVITABLE PART OF THIS PROCESS.
I WISH I COULD SAY I WAS SORRY, BUT I'VE LIED TO YOU ENOUGH. AND AT THIS POINT...
THE TRUTH HURTS MORE THAN A LIE, DOESN'T IT?
NO--NOBODY WILL PUT UP WITH ME, NOT LIKE THIS... I WON'T EVEN BE ABLE TO FIND A JOB...
YOU'LL NEVER BE ABLE TO HIDE YOUR PAST. NOBODY WILL WANT TO BE WITH YOU.

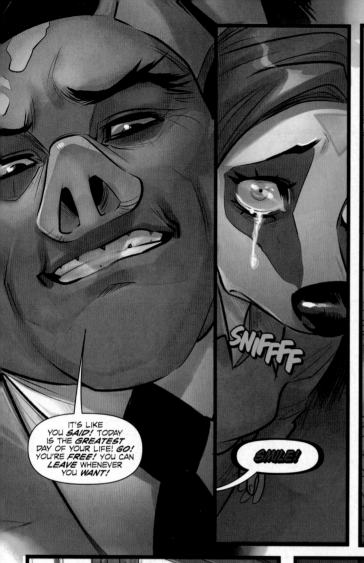

IT'S LIKE YOU *SAID!* TODAY IS THE *GREATEST* DAY OF YOUR LIFE! *GO!* YOU'RE *FREE!* YOU CAN *LEAVE* WHENEVER YOU *WANT!*

SNIFFF

SMILE!

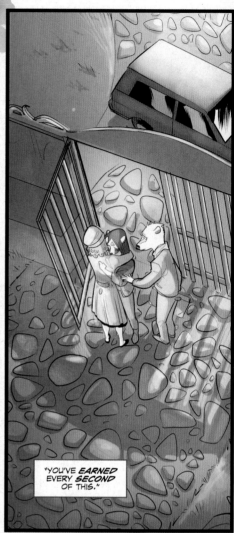

"YOU'VE *EARNED* EVERY *SECOND* OF THIS."

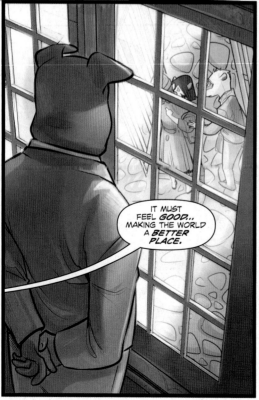

IT MUST FEEL *GOOD...* MAKING THE WORLD A *BETTER* PLACE.

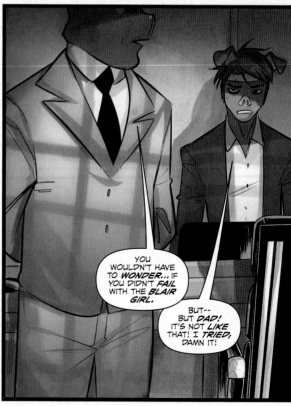

YOU WOULDN'T HAVE TO *WONDER...* IF YOU DIDN'T *FAIL* WITH THE *BLAIR GIRL.*

BUT-- BUT *DAD!* IT'S NOT *LIKE* THAT! I *TRIED,* DAMN IT!

DO NOT CALL ME "DAD"!
YOU CAN USE THAT WORD WHEN YOU'RE NOT TRADING OFF YOUR LINEAGE FOR FORGIVENESS.
WE'D HAVE ENORMOUS POWER RIGHT NOW...IF NOT FOR YOU.
WE WILL HAVE IT!
TZZ
I HOPE SO, JONES... FAMILY OR NOT, YOU'RE TESTING MY PATIENCE.
DON'T SAY THAT, DAD...WE'LL TURN THIS AROUND. I HEARD THE GLANCE HAS GOOD NEWS.
LESLIE BLAIR IS NOW ON THE RUN FOR A DOUBLE HOMICIDE ONLY WE KNOW SHE DIDN'T COMMIT. HER ESCAPE FROM THE POLICE ONLY HELPED US. "IF SHE WERE INNOCENT, WHY WOULD SHE RUN?"
THE LEADER NOW ANSWERS TO US. CONTROLLING HIM WAS EASIER THAN EXPECTED...

YOU WERE RIGHT, JONES. THIS IS GOOD NEWS.
WE'VE GIVEN THE ORDER TO HUNT BLAIR DOWN. NO CLUE IS TOO SMALL.
OUR AGENTS ALREADY TURNED UP THAT PET OF HERS, THANKS TO CCTV.
UNFORTUNATELY, WE FOUND THE FOOTAGE TOO LATE.
IT WOULD BE EASIER TO HUNT IF OUR CONTROL EXTENDED BEYOND THE CITY LIMITS...
WE'RE WORKING ON THAT.
IN THE MEANTIME... WHAT ABOUT THE VAN THAT BLAIR ESCAPED IN? WERE WE ABLE TO IDENTIFY IT?
NO...
AND WE KNOW NOTHING ABOUT THE WOLF THAT HELPED HER. HIS STRENGTH ALONE IS... INTRIGUING.
WHAT DO YOU MEAN?
JUST AS LESLIE BLAIR RESEMBLES THE BES OF MYTH...
THIS WHITE WOLF CAN'T BE A COINCIDENCE.
I DON'T CARE WHO THE BASTARD LOOKS LIKE. ALL I KNOW IS, WHEN I FIND HIM...

"HE'LL REGRET LEAVING ME ALIVE."
I...I CAN STILL FEEL HIM...INSIDE OF ME...
WHAT DOES IT FEEL LIKE?
A KIND OF STRENGTH... BUT IT'S LIKE A BURDEN...
I CAN FEEL A...A POWER STRUGGLING TO OVERTAKE ME.
THAT IS EXACTLY WHAT THE ALBINO IS, LESLIE.
HE'S A PRIMORDIAL FORCE THAT CAN POSSESS YOU, LEAVING YOU A PRISONER IN YOUR OWN BODY.
BUT-- BUT CAROL, WHO IS THE ALBINO? DID HE DO THAT TO ME? AND IF--IF HE DID...
...WHY AM I STILL ALIVE?
BES.
THAT NAME...
HE CALLED ME THAT...LIKE HE KNEW HER, YEAH...FROM A LONG TIME AGO.

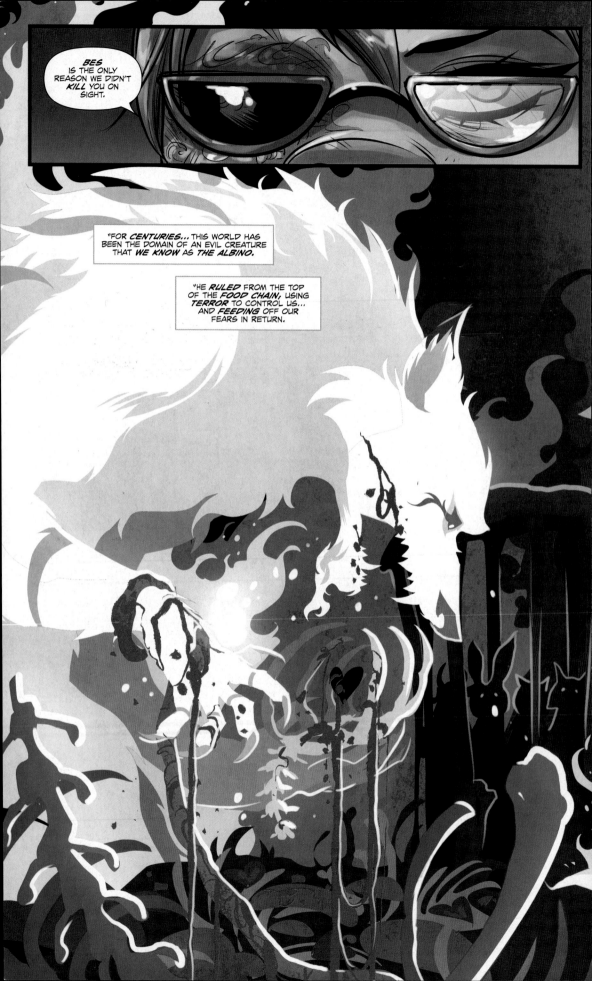

BES IS THE ONLY REASON WE DIDN'T **KILL** YOU ON SIGHT.

"FOR **CENTURIES...** THIS WORLD HAS BEEN THE DOMAIN OF AN EVIL CREATURE THAT **WE KNOW** AS **THE ALBINO.**

"HE **RULED** FROM THE TOP OF THE **FOOD CHAIN,** USING **TERROR** TO CONTROL US... AND **FEEDING** OFF OUR FEARS IN RETURN.

"AND YET...HE DIDN'T HAVE **EVERYTHING.** MORTALS HAD SOMETHING HE **NEVER COULD.** FOR ALL HIS **POWER...** HE WAS **ALONE.**

"SO, THE INHABITANTS OF **TIJOUX** OFFERED HIM A PACT: THEY WOULD MAKE **OFFERINGS,** WOMEN FOR HIM TO **LOVE...** IN RETURN FOR THEIR **SAFETY.**

"THE **SACRIFICES** MADE THEMSELVES KNOWN IN DIFFERENT WAYS. **BLUE HAIR,** FOR EXAMPLE, WAS A SIGN OF BEING **PREDESTINED** FOR THE ALBINO.

"WHEN HER TIME CAME, **BES** COULDN'T ACCEPT THIS FATE. SHE DID SOMETHING **MIRACULOUS.** SHE **REBELLED.**

"SHE **REFUSED** TO BE SACRIFICED TO THE **ALBINO'S LUST...** BECAUSE SHE SECRETLY ALREADY **HAD** A **PARTNER** AND A **FAMILY.**

"BES WASN'T LIKE THE **OTHERS...** BUT **YOU** ARE LIKE **BES.** IN FACT, LESLIE... WE THINK YOU **ARE** BES. AND WE'VE GOT **PLANS** FOR YOU."

DO YOU NOW?
YOU KNOW NOTHING ABOUT OUR PAST, MORTAL!
UH?
BES LOVED ME.
SHE WAS NO MERE SACRIFICE. SHE WAS MORE. I WANTED TO BE WITH HER... BE ONE WITH HER!
BUT NOT LIKE THIS...NOT IN A FORM SO WEAK...
NOT TRAPPED IN THIS LESSER BODY.
OH YEAH? YOU LOVE HER, SO YOU ENSLAVE HER SOUL, YOU MONSTER?
YOU CAN GO TO HELL!
STMHP

TRHUM
I GROW TIRED OF THIS FORM... BUT EVERY MOMENT THAT PASSES BRINGS ME CLOSER TO MY AWAKENING!
AND THERE IS NOTHING YOU CAN DO TO STOP IT!
STOP!
YOU HEARD THEM! STOP, PLEASE!
STOP RUNNING!
SHUT UP, GIRL!
I MUST ESCAPE! THERE MUST BE A WAY...
I CAN'T THINK WITH YOUR CONSTANT CRYING IN MY HEAD! BE SILENT!
NO... NO! I WANT TO STAY HERE!
FOOLISH GIRL! IF YOU'D JUST STOP RESISTING...
I KNOW... I KNOW YOU STILL LOVE ME...

LESLIE!
IT'S OKAY, I THINK YOU'RE BACK TO BEING... YOU. LISTEN TO ME. THERE'S INCREDIBLE POWER INSIDE OF YOU. AND I'M NOT TALKING ABOUT THE ALBINOS... I'M TALKING ABOUT BES.
YOU ARE BES. HER BLOOD FLOWS IN YOUR VEINS. AND I AM NOT GOING TO LET THE SAVIOR OF THE WORLD DIE... NOT AGAIN!
Y-YOU'LL... HELP ME TO GET RID OF HIM?
I WILL. TOMORROW WE LEAVE FOR TIJOUX, WHERE THE REMAINS OF THE ORIGINAL BES REST.
COMMUNING WITH THEM WILL ALIGN HER POWER INSIDE YOU. IT WILL BE COMPLETE... ENOUGH TO DESTROY THE ALBINO ONCE AND FOR ALL.
I GAVE UP YEARS OF MY LIFE STUDYING TIJOUX, STUDYING YOU... YOU CAN TRUST ME.
WHAT--WHAT ABOUT JONES AND HIS GANG? WHAT DO THEY WANT FROM ME?
THEY WANT TO STEAL THE ALBINO'S POWER FROM WITHIN YOUR BODY. YOU HAVE NO IDEA WHAT HE'S CAPABLE OF.
WHAT THEY HAVE PLANNED FOR THAT POWER... THE REPRODUCTION PROGRAM, THE LAWS...
THEY'RE JUST THE TIP OF THE ICEBERG. AND BENEATH THE SURFACE... IT'S TERRIFYING.
BUT... YOU'VE HAD A LONG DAY. YOU SHOULD REST.
RIGHT NOW... I THINK YOU'RE TOO SHAKEN FOR THE WHOLE TRUTH.
THERE'S PLENTY OF TIME FOR EXPLANATIONS.
BUT... I...
MPHF!

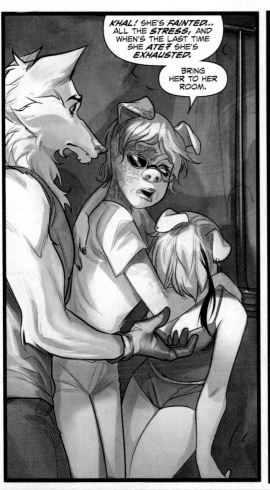

KHAL! SHE'S **FAINTED**... ALL THE **STRESS**, AND WHEN'S THE LAST TIME SHE **ATE?** SHE'S **EXHAUSTED.**

BRING HER TO HER ROOM.

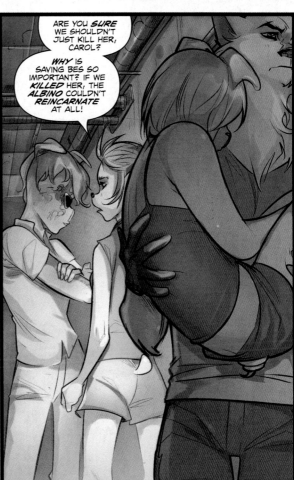

ARE YOU **SURE** WE SHOULDN'T JUST KILL HER, CAROL?

WHY IS SAVING BES SO IMPORTANT? IF WE **KILLED** HER, THE **ALBINO** COULDN'T **REINCARNATE** AT ALL!

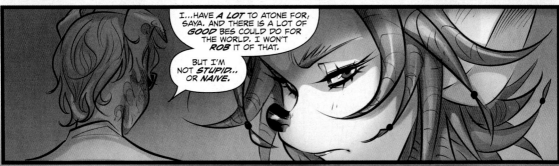

I...HAVE **A LOT** TO ATONE FOR, SAYA. AND THERE IS A LOT OF **GOOD** BES COULD DO FOR THE WORLD. I WON'T **ROB** IT OF THAT.

BUT I'M NOT **STUPID**... OR **NAIVE.**

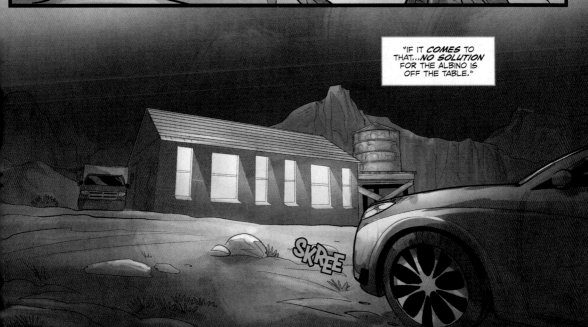

"IF IT **COMES** TO THAT...**NO SOLUTION** FOR THE ALBINO IS OFF THE TABLE."

SKREE

DUN DLON
...YES?
I'M SORRY, SIR. BUT OUR CAR BROKE DOWN, AND MY FRIENDS AND I'VE GOT NO CELL SERVICE...
WE SAW YOUR PLACE, AND YOU LOOK LIKE A KIND MAN...
"DO YOU THINK YOU COULD HELP US?"
I'M...I'M SCARED, KHAL! WILL YOU STAY WITH ME?
...NO.
PLEASE! YOU CAN'T LEAVE!
I SAID NO!

DON'T TALK TO ME LIKE THAT, ASSHOLE!
YOU'VE GOT NO IDEA WHAT I'VE BEEN THROUGH!
JUST STOP!
I KNOW SAYA TOLD YOU ABOUT ME! SO, YOU WANT TO TALK ABOUT SUFFERING, PRINCESS?
GET IN LINE.
I--I'M SORRY, KHAL. YOU'RE RIGHT, I...
I'M THE ONE THAT'S SORRY.
I CAN'T PROTECT YOU FROM THE ALBINO, HE'S ALREADY INSIDE YOU. THE ONLY PERSON THAT CAN HELP YOU...
...IS YOU!

BUT I'M... I'M JUST A NORMAL GIRL! I--I CAN'T DO THIS!
I'M NOT STRONG ENOUGH! HE...
SOB
SNFF
HE NEVER LEAVES ME ALONE, KHAL.
THE ALBINO'S ALWAYS IN THERE... TRYING TO TAKE OVER MY HEAD AGAIN.
I KNOW HE IS, LESLIE.
THAT'S MY LEGACY. YOU KNOW THAT, RIGHT?
I CAN SEE THE ALBINO.
I SEE HIM THERE, ALWAYS TORMENTING YOU. TAUNTING YOU.
I ALSO SEE THAT HE'S STILL WEAK. HE DOESN'T HAVE A BODY OF HIS OWN... NOT YET.
YOU COULD STILL DO IT. YOU COULD STOP HIM.
"STILL WEAK"? IT IS NOT WISE TO UNDERESTIMATE ME, GREAT-GRANDSON...

HEY... MAYBE I DO HAVE SOMETHING THAT'LL HELP.
SWIISH
?
TAK
CAROL SAID SHE'S BEEN STUDYING YOU, AND SHE WASN'T LYING.
SHE THOUGHT YOU MIGHT LIKE SOME BLACK LIPSTICK... TO REMIND YOU OF TRISH.
YOUR FRIENDS MIGHT BE GONE, BUT TAKE IT FROM ME, LESLIE...
THE HAPPY MOMENTS YOU HAD WITH THEM NEVER HAVE TO DIE.
CHERISH THEM. USE THEM. TAKE STRENGTH IN THEM...
YOU'LL NEED IT FOR THE FIGHT AHEAD.

MY DREAMS, AFTER ALL THIS...
ZZZ
Z-ZZZZ
THEY'RE STRANGER THAN EVER.
MY MEMORIES SEEM... SHARPER AFTER THIS "AWAKENING" RITUAL.
I REMEMBER FLASHES, SMALL DETAILS...MEMORIES FROM TWO DIFFERENT LIVES... BUT THEY'RE BOTH ME.
IN MY PAST LIFE THERE WAS NOTHING THAT SCARED ME, EXCEPT, I THINK, MY FEELINGS. BECAUSE IN THAT LIFE...
THEY WERE REAL.

I USED TO THINK MY BIGGEST PROBLEM WAS LOVING A MAN FROM A DIFFERENT SPECIES. WHAT AN IDIOT!
CAROL SAYS JONES AND HIS GANG WANT TO KEEP US APART... BUT WHY? WHAT'S THE REAL REASON THE REPRODUCTION PROGRAM EXISTS?
WHY DO THEY SPY ON EVERYONE AND EVERYTHING?
WHO IS "THE GLANCE"? I KNOW HE'S BEHIND THIS, SOMEHOW; HE'S BEHIND EVERYTHING...
BUT WHY? WHY IS HE SO DESPERATE TO JUDGE ME?
WHAT?! BEHIND THE MASK-- YOU!
WHY IS IT ME THAT ALWAYS HAS TO BE TORMENTED LIKE THIS?

BECAUSE I WANT YOU ALL FOR MYSELF...
MY SWEET, HELPLESS BRIDE!
MAN, LESLIE...HOW MUCH DO YOU WEIGH?
SEE? WE'RE HERE FOR YOU, LIKE ALWAYS...
DEREK! TRISH! I DON'T BELIEVE IT! YOU SAVED ME! YOU--
LESLIE!
SOMEHOW THEY FOUND US! IF YOU WANT TO LIVE... WE'VE GOT TO GO! NOW!

CHAPTER
SEVEN

LET'S GO! SEARCH EVERYWHERE!
THOSE DEGENERATES ARE HERE! THEY HAVE TO BE...
SIR!
I THINK I FOUND SOMETHING.
UNLESS I'M THE ONLY ONE WHO DOESN'T KEEP HIS STAIRS BEHIND HIS CLOSET... WE'VE GOT THEM.
GET DOWN THERE. BUT KEEP QUIET.
I WANT COMPLETE SILENCE...
"I WANT TO SURPRISE THIS FILTH."
TAP

EEEEEEE--
WHAT'S HAPPENING, CAROL?
THAT'S--THAT'S RICK'S ALARM SIGNAL! IF HE TRIGGERED IT, THAT MEANS...
SOMEONE FOUND US!
OKAY, OKAY, STAY CALM... ALL THIS MEANS IS WE'RE LEAVING SOONER THAN WE PLANNED.
BUT WE DO HAVE A PLAN.
SKREEEEK
THIS WAY, QUICKLY! YOU KNOW WHAT TO DO.
SAYA! KHAL! TAKE LESLIE!
FOLLOW THEM, LESLIE. IT'S GOING TO BE OKAY, I PROMISE.
OKAY, YEAH. OKAY...
BANG
CAMERON!

NOOOO!

CAROL!

GO! DON'T STOP! YOU'VE GOT TO--

YOU SHUT UP!

LET'S GO! FOLLOW THEM!

AND LISTEN TO ME. THIS "CAROL" BETTER BE ALIVE WHEN I GET BACK.

AS YOU WISH, JONES, SIR!

THEY'RE GETTING AWAY!

NO, THEY'RE NOT.

BANG

ZIING

AAH!

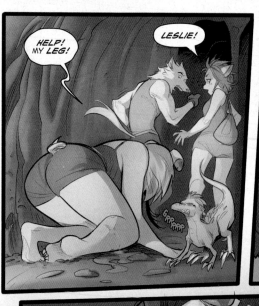

HELP! MY LEG!

LESLIE!

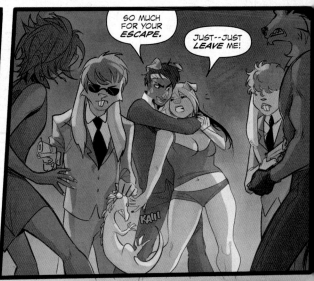

SO MUCH FOR YOUR ESCAPE.

JUST--JUST LEAVE ME!

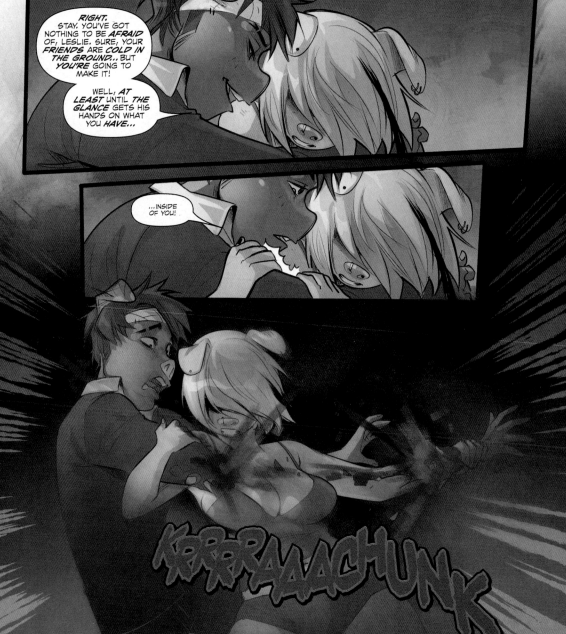

RIGHT. STAY. YOU'VE GOT NOTHING TO BE AFRAID OF, LESLIE. SURE, YOUR FRIENDS ARE COLD IN THE GROUND... BUT YOU'RE GOING TO MAKE IT!

WELL, AT LEAST UNTIL THE GLANCE GETS HIS HANDS ON WHAT YOU HAVE...

...INSIDE OF YOU!

KRRRAAACHUNK

!
TMP
IT IS BEST...
...TO STAY AWAY FROM US!
I AM NO MERE INSTRUMENT FOR FILTHY MORTAL WHIMS!
YOUR PATHETIC QUARRELS MEAN NOTHING TO ME! ALMOST AS LITTLE...
...AS YOUR USELESS LIVES!
DO IT, LESLIE! KILL THIS SCUM!
I--I DON'T KNOW IF I CAN...
DO IT NOW! HE MURDERED YOUR KIN!

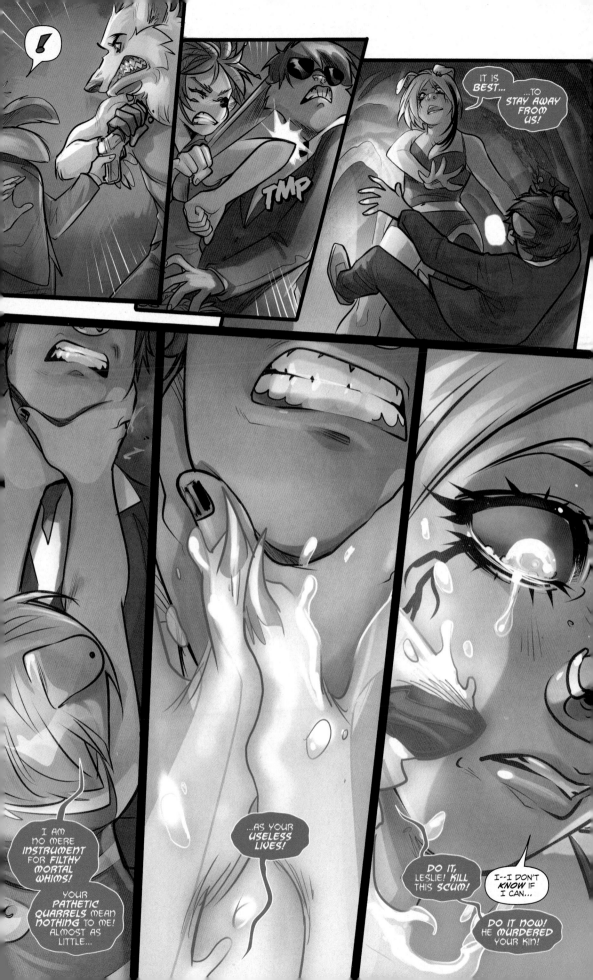

NO! NO! NO!
I CAN'T KILL SOMEONE, EVEN FOR THAT! I'M NOT LIKE YOU!
NO TIME TO ARGUE!
LET'S GO!
NO! NO!
NO!
NO!

THEY'RE DISTRACTED DEALING WITH THAT PIG'S ARM...WE COULD GO BACK FOR CAROL...
SHE TOLD US TO GO, SAYA. IT'S--IT'S OKAY. THEY WON'T KILL HER, SHE KNOWS TOO MUCH THAT THEY DON'T.
I KNOW, KHAL...
"THAT'S EXACTLY WHAT I'M AFRAID OF."
VROOOOOM
PLIC
PLIC
PLIC
PLIC
PLIC

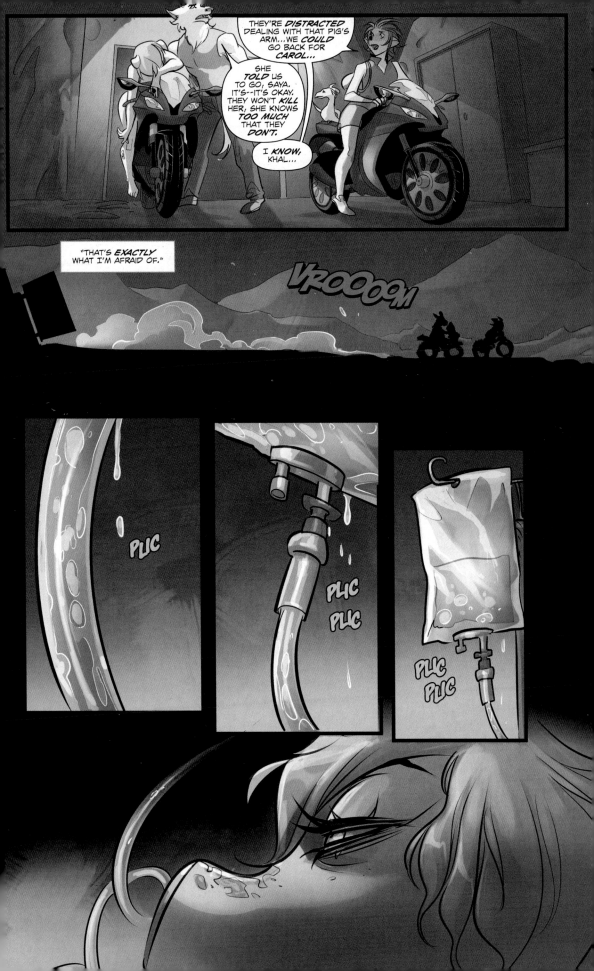

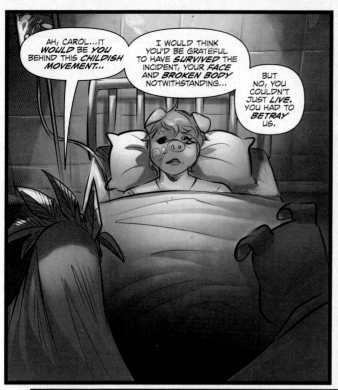

AH, CAROL...IT *WOULD* BE *YOU* BEHIND THIS *CHILDISH* MOVEMENT...

I WOULD THINK YOU'D BE GRATEFUL TO HAVE *SURVIVED* THE INCIDENT; YOUR *FACE* AND *BROKEN BODY* NOTWITHSTANDING...

BUT NO, YOU COULDN'T JUST *LIVE.* YOU HAD TO *BETRAY* US.

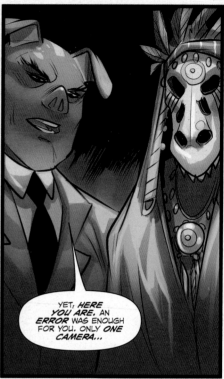

YET, *HERE YOU ARE.* AN *ERROR* WAS ENOUGH FOR YOU. ONLY *ONE* CAMERA...

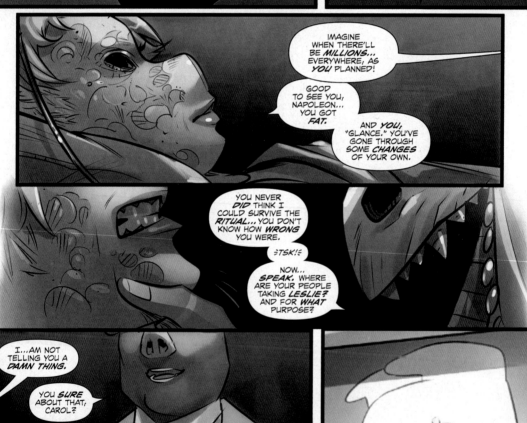

IMAGINE WHEN THERE'LL BE *MILLIONS*... EVERYWHERE, AS *YOU* PLANNED!

GOOD TO SEE YOU, NAPOLEON... YOU GOT *FAT.*

AND *YOU,* "GLANCE." YOU'VE GONE THROUGH SOME *CHANGES* OF YOUR OWN.

YOU NEVER *DID* THINK I COULD SURVIVE THE *RITUAL*...YOU DON'T KNOW HOW *WRONG* YOU WERE.

≶TSK!≶

NOW... *SPEAK.* WHERE ARE YOUR PEOPLE TAKING *LESLIE?* AND FOR *WHAT* PURPOSE?

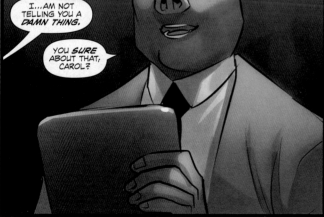

I...AM NOT TELLING YOU A *DAMN THING.*

YOU *SURE* ABOUT THAT, CAROL?

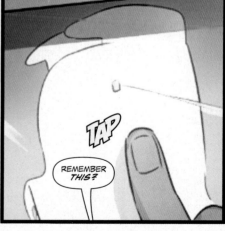

TAP

REMEMBER *THIS?*

AAAAAH!
THAT... THAT CAN'T BE MY--
BUT IT IS. YOU'RE ENJOYING THE VERY DEVICE YOU YOURSELF DESIGNED BEFORE WE...PARTED WAYS.
TAP
I CAN'T LIE, YOU'RE GOING TO HATE IT HERE AT THE SLAUGHTERHOUSE...
NNNGH!
BUT IT'S WHERE YOU'RE GOING TO STAY...

"...UNTIL YOU'RE NO LONGER OF USE TO US."
I FEEL RIDICULOUS DRESSED LIKE THIS, SAYA.
YOU'RE A WANTED PIG, STUPID!
THANKFULLY, CAROL LEFT US SOME CASH OR WE'D BE ON THE STREET.
MOTEL
POOL!
LET'S SEE, YOU SAID...A ROOM FOR THREE? YOU'RE ALL OF YOU... WHAT'S THE POLITE PHRASE THESE DAYS... TOGETHER?
THAT'S NONE OF YOUR BUSINESS, YOU OLD DOG!
WELL, ACTUALLY... IT IS.
THERE ARE LAWS. I DON'T WANT TO GO TO JAIL.
READ THE SIGN--WE DON'T RENT TO PERVERTS.
MIXED COUPLES
COME ON, GUYS. WE CAN FIND ANOTHER ROOM.
CALM DOWN, LESLIE. YOU THINK THIS IDIOT REALLY CARES ABOUT THAT? HE'S JUST GOING THROUGH THE MOTIONS.
I KNOW WHAT YOU WANT. I'M SORRY FOR LOSING MY TEMPER. WILL THIS BE ENOUGH, CONSIDERING THE...BOTHER?
THAT...WILL DO. BARELY. BUT LISTEN...
WE DON'T GET MANY CUSTOMERS. IT'S HARD TO GO UNNOTICED THESE DAYS.
BUT TRY, OKAY?
OF COURSE, SIR...
FZZZZ
FOR ALL OUR SAKES.

COME ON, YOU SELFISH SWINE! LET'S *MOVE IT ALONG!*

IT'S MY TURN!

TOC TOC TOC

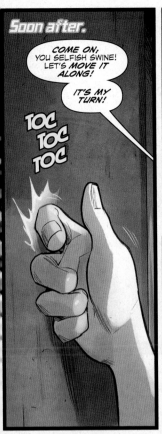

IT'S BEEN A *SHITTY DAY*... CAN I *AT LEAST* GO TO THE *BATHROOM* BEFORE I EXPLODE?

ENOUGH, SAYA! I DON'T NEED THE DETAILS!

EASY FOR *YOU* TO SAY! *YOU'VE* ALREADY SHOWERED, KHAL!

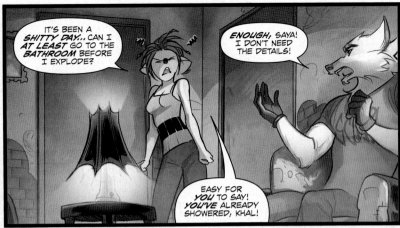

COME TO *THINK* OF IT, *YOU* TOOK FOREVER TOO!

MY WHOLE *BODY'S* COVERED IN *FUR.* IT DOESN'T JUST MAGICALLY *DRY* IN AN INSTANT.

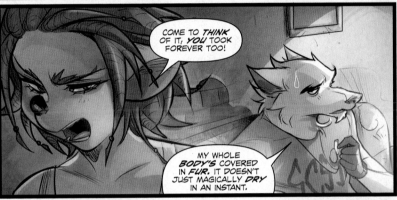

HERE, SAYA! GO AHEAD.

ABOUT TIME!

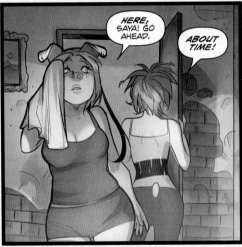

SAYA'S RANT...SHE'S JUST *WORRIED* ABOUT CAROL, RIGHT?

WE *ALL* ARE, LESLIE.

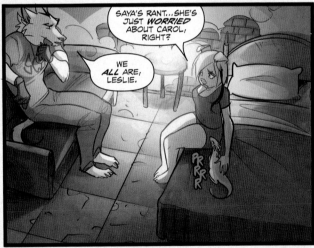

I'M EVEN *MORE* WORRIED THAN SAYA, HONESTLY.

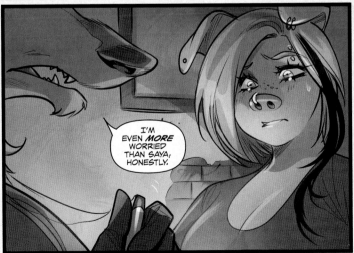

KHAL...THAT *THING* AROUND YOUR NECK, CAN I ASK YOU WHAT IT DOES?

IT SEEMS LIKE *MAYBE*...IT *JAMS* TECHNOLOGY? LIKE *CAMERAS?*

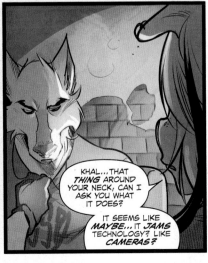

DEAD ON.
THE GLANCE HAS SURVEILLANCE ALL OVER NEW ROARK. BUT I CAN'T USE THE NECKLACE ALL THE TIME. THEY'D NOTICE IF THERE WERE TOO MANY DISRUPTIONS IN THEIR DATA FEED. AN ALARM WOULD TRIP AND JUST LIKE THAT... THEY'D FIND US.
AT YOUR FRIEND DEREK'S PLACE, I DIDN'T HAVE A CHOICE. PLUS, THEY ALREADY KNEW WHERE WE WERE.
BUT...WHY DO YOU DO ALL THIS? I DON'T UNDERSTAND...
YOU TRUST CAROL THAT MUCH? SHE'S NOT EXACTLY FORTHCOMING WITH HER MOTIVATIONS.
NOT WITH YOU. YOU'RE NOT READY. WITHOUT CAROL, SAYA WOULD BE ON THE STREET. AND ME? I'D BE...WELL, YOU KNOW WHAT I'D BE.
THE REPRODUCTION PROGRAM IS A FARCE. I JUST KNOW IT. ALL THEY REALLY WANT TO DO IS SPREAD HATE.
AND YOU KNOW WHAT? AS LONG AS MY SISTER'S SAFE...I'M HAPPY, NO MATTER WHERE I AM OR WHAT I'M DOING.
WHERE IS SHE NOW? YOU MISS HER?
I MISS SHEA SO MUCH...IT'S BEEN YEARS SINCE I'VE SEEN HER. CAROL SET HER UP TO LIVE WITH A NICE, SAFE FAMILY.
KHAL! SHE'S SO CUUUTE!
CHILL. YOU'RE FREAKING ME OUT WITH THAT LOOK ON YOUR FACE.
SHEA'S SMART. SHE KNOWS THAT IF WE'RE APART, IT'S FOR A GOOD REASON. IT'S-- IT'S ENOUGH TO KNOW SHE'S SAFE AND HAPPY. WHEN I MISS HER, I'VE STILL GOT HER PICTURES...

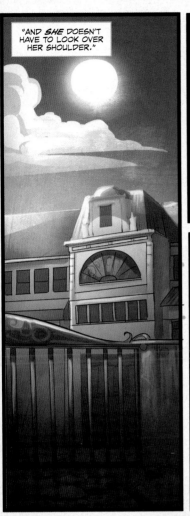

"AND *SHE* DOESN'T HAVE TO LOOK OVER HER SHOULDER."

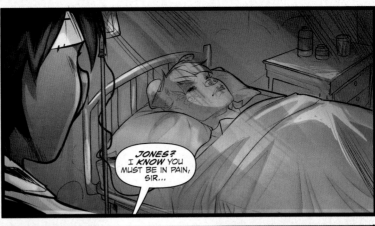

JONES? I *KNOW* YOU MUST BE IN PAIN, SIR...

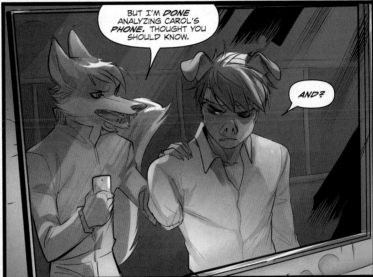

BUT I'M *DONE* ANALYZING CAROL'S *PHONE.* THOUGHT YOU SHOULD KNOW.

AND?

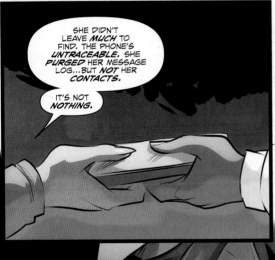

SHE DIDN'T LEAVE *MUCH* TO FIND. THE PHONE'S *UNTRACEABLE.* SHE *PURGED* HER MESSAGE LOG...BUT *NOT* HER CONTACTS.

IT'S NOT *NOTHING.*

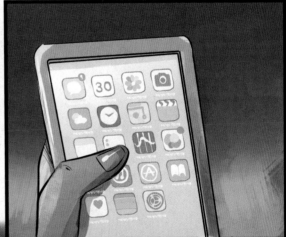

YOU'RE RIGHT.

LET'S SEND SOME *MESSAGES* OUT INTO THE WORLD...

"AND SEE WHO'S LISTENING."
PLIC PLIC
...NO.
THOSE BASTARDS.
NO, NO...
CAROL...
Messages
Carol
Details
Where are you? If you want Carol to remain unharmed, you'll tell me, and quickly...
I...I CAN'T.
THE MISSION... IT'S MORE IMPORTANT. THAT'S WHAT CAROL WOULD SAY.
I...CAN'T...
I CAN'T...

SO...YEAH, IT WAS AT THAT MOMENT I REALIZED I HAD WAY TOO MUCH FUR AND WAS WAY TOO CLOSE TO THE FIREPLACE.
AHAH!
I DID FINALLY GET A SMILE OUT OF YOU.
IT'S BEEN...A MINUTE SINCE I LAUGHED. I THINK I OWE YOU AN APOLOGY, KHAL. YOU HAVE BEEN KIND TO ME, IN YOUR OWN WAY.
AND YOU'RE RIGHT ABOUT A LOT. LIKE IT OR NOT...I'VE GOT THIS THING, THE ALBINO, INSIDE OF ME...
AND IF I LET MY GUARD DOWN, EVEN FOR A SECOND...I COULD LOSE MYSELF.
I DON'T WANT TO CHANGE. I DON'T WANT TO LET THE ALBINO TURN ME INTO SOMETHING I'M NOT... SOME KIND OF ASSASSIN.
LESLIE...
YOU ARE STRONG. MORE THAN YOU KNOW.
AND I'M WITH YOU.
I WON'T LET THAT BASTARD TURN YOU INTO ANYTHING, YOU HEAR ME?
I PROMISE!

ENOUGH, YOU TWO! I'M GETTING DIABETES OVER HERE...
IF YOU WANT A ROOM ALONE THAT BAD, JUST SAY IT.
SBAM
?
IT'S NOT WHAT YOU THINK...
AS IF I WOULD FUCKING THINK ABOUT IT AT ALL...
IF I WERE YOU, I'D BE DOING MORE SLEEPING AND LESS FLIRTING...
"WE'VE GOT A LONG ROAD AHEAD."
BRIDE...
BRIDE...
BRIDE...
LET US GO! NOW!

LEAVE ME ALONE, DAMN IT! AT LEAST LET ME SLEEP...
YOU MAY BE ASLEEP, BUT I'M AWAKE. I CAN SENSE MUCH, MY BRIDE, AND I SHOULD TELL YOU...
WE ARE NOT GOING TO BE ALONE FOR LONG.
GOOD WORK. YOU'RE RIGHT...IT'S HER. NOW...
ROUND THEM UP.
AAAH!
UH?

GRRR!
THMP
AAAH!
LET ME OUT, BRIDE...LET ME ACT, FOR BOTH OUR SAKES!
N-NO...
NO!
ARGH!
DO YOU KNOW HOW MUCH THEY'LL PAY FOR YOU?
LESLIE!

THERE, THE CAR!
HELP!
ALONE IN A ROOM WITH A WOLF AND A HEDGEHOG...
YOU REALLY ARE A NASTY ONE!
THEY SAY PEOPLE LIKE YOU WILL FUCK ANYTHING.
I SAY SOMEONE NEEDS TO TEACH YOU ABOUT RIGHT AND WRONG...
ACCEPTABLE AND UNACCEPTABLE... NATURAL AND UNNATURAL...
I'LL TEACH YOU, LITTLE PIG, WITH EXTREME PREJUDICE...
!
NO!

SCRAAAAH
no one will HARM you, my bride.
no one TOUCHES us...
no one!
TAP
Messages
Carol
Where are you? If you want Carol to remain unharmed, you'll tell me, and quickly...
SENDING MESSAGE IN PROGRESS...

CHAPTER EIGHT

Tijoux
I THINK... I'LL TAKE THIS, TOO!
THANK YOU! AND HAVE A GREAT HOLIDAY!
HOLIDAY...?
"I WISH..."

UFF
I'LL MAKE YOU PAY FOR THIS! DO YOU HEAR ME IN THERE, ALBINO? YOU WON'T GET AWAY WITH WHAT YOU'VE DONE TO LESLIE!
I'LL TAKE YOUR LIFE LONG BEFORE THAT, MORTAL POSEUR. IT WILL BE MY FIRST ACT ONCE ME AND MY BRIDE HERE ARE UNITED AS ONE.
THAT--THAT WON'T HAPPEN! I WON'T LET IT!
YOUR WORD MEANS NOTHING, FOOL...EVEN LESLIE AGREES, I CAN HEAR IT IN HER HEAD.
I...
I'LL MAKE YOU EAT THOSE WORDS, YOU--
ENOUGH! JUST STOP, PLEASE!

IT'S USELESS TO YELL, KHAL... THE ALBINO'S ALREADY WON. IT'S OVER!
BULLSHIT, LESLIE! ONCE WE GET TO TIJOUX, EVERYTHING WILL BE FINE...
HE'S ONLY WON IF YOU LET THAT BE TRUE.
IT'S A NICE IDEA... BUT HE'S RIGHT. YOU'VE MADE A LOT OF PROMISES BEFORE, AND I'M TIRED. OF THEM...
...OF EVERYTHING.
I GOT EVERYTHING! LET'S GO! THE CLOCK'S TICKING...
"...AND I'M WORRIED ABOUT CAROL. EVERY MINUTE SHE'S A PRISONER OF THE REPRODUCTION INITIATIVE COULD BE HER LAST."
CRD
WHAT'S WRONG, SWEETHEART? YOU MISS HOME?

I'M SORRY, BUT YOU REALLY CAN'T GO BACK... EVER.
IT'S FOR YOUR OWN GOOD! WE TELL ALL OUR PATIENTS THE SAME THING!
MY OWN GOOD? YOU DON'T KNOW ME.
YOU PROBABLY DON'T EVEN KNOW WHY I'M HERE, NOT REALLY...
I DON'T HAVE TO KNOW. I DON'T CARE. YOU PERVERTS ARE ALL THE SAME! I'VE SEEN A THOUSAND!
YOUR... UNNATURAL INCLINATIONS MUST BE FOUGHT WITH STRONG DISCIPLINE, TIME AND PATIENCE!
RIGHT NOW, YOU'RE WEAK. YOUR LUST RUNS YOUR LIFE. EVEN NOW...EVEN IN THIS MOMENT, I BET YOU CAN'T HELP BUT WANT ME. RIGHT?
SORRY... BUT WITH AN ASS THAT FLAT? YOU'RE NOT MY TYPE, SIS.
THROO
FUCK YOU!
ENOUGH, NURSE!

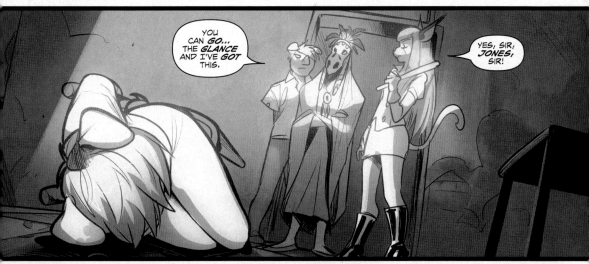

YOU CAN *GO*... THE *GLANCE* AND I'VE *GOT* THIS.

YES, SIR, *JONES*, SIR!

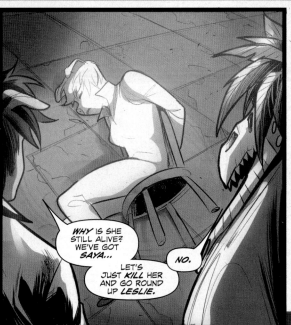

WHY IS SHE STILL ALIVE? WE'VE GOT *SAYA*...

NO.

LET'S JUST *KILL* HER AND GO ROUND UP *LESLIE*.

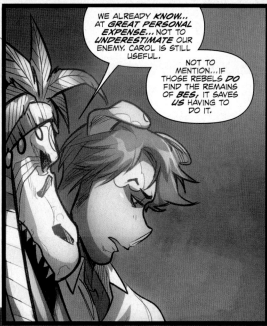

WE ALREADY *KNOW*... AT *GREAT PERSONAL EXPENSE*... NOT TO *UNDERESTIMATE* OUR ENEMY. CAROL IS STILL USEFUL.

NOT TO MENTION...IF THOSE REBELS *DO* FIND THE REMAINS OF *BES*, IT SAVES *US* HAVING TO DO IT.

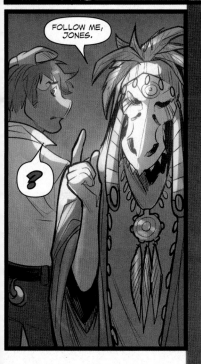

FOLLOW ME, JONES.

?

I'M...NOT SURE I *AGREE* WITH KEEPING CAROL ALIVE. BUT IF YOU *SAY* IT'S THE BEST PLAY, I *TRUST* YOU. IT'S JUST...I DON'T FEEL LIKE SHE'S MUCH OF AN ACE IN THE HOLE.

THIS IS *BEST*, BUT IT'S NOT *ALL*. YOU *KNOW* I DON'T LEAVE ANYTHING TO *CHANCE*, JONES.

DO YOU *REALLY* THINK...

"...I ONLY HAVE ONE ACE TO PLAY?"
ZAC
IF THIS MAP IS RIGHT...WE'RE CLOSE TO TIJOUX.
UHM...
WHAT'S WRONG, KHAL?
SO FOR GENERATIONS, TIJOUX IS OFF THE MAP. NO CONTACT WITH CIVILIZATION AT ALL... AND NOW?
THEY'VE GOT MAPS... POSTCARDS?
YOU'RE RIGHT...
THIS HAS BEEN TOO EASY.
THINGS CHANGE OVER TIME...BUT NOT THIS MUCH.
Tijoux
WELCOME
NO KIDDING. THIS IS DEFINITELY NEW AND DEFINITELY...
...WEIRD?
?

TIJOUX PARK
SOUVENIRS
BAR
IS THIS A JOKE?!
SOUVENIRS
WHAT IS THIS SHIT?
AND WHERE ARE THE PEOPLE?
KHAL...I'M SORRY.
I DIDN'T THINK MUCH OF THESE PEOPLE...BUT HOW COULD THEY SELL OUT SO BADLY? HOW COULD THEY LET THEM TURN OUR LAND, OUR HOME... INTO SOME TOURIST FREAKSHOW?!
LET'S...TRY TO MAKE THAT GLASS HALF FULL, YEAH?
IF TIJOUX ISN'T SOME LONG-LOST VILLAGE SHROUDED IN MYSTERY... MAYBE IT'LL BE EASIER FOR US TO FIND WHAT WE'RE HERE FOR.
HELLO, FRIENDS! YOU SEEM PERPLEXED... SEARCHING FOR ANSWERS? OR, PERHAPS, SOME HALF-PRICED SNACKS? THEN I'M YOUR MAN! SO LONG AS YOU PROMISE NOT TO CHECK THE EXPIRATION DATES.

THAT'S RIGHT! THE SOLUTION TO ALL YOUR PROBLEMS. YOUR GUIDE TO TIJOUX...
I'M KIRK! AND I'M A BIT RUSTY, SURE...BUT I'M BETTER THAN NOTHING!
I SHOULD ALSO POINT OUT...I'M YOUR ONLY CHOICE!
CLOSED
EXPLAIN... "A BIT RUSTY."
WELL, THIS PLACE HASN'T SEEN BUSINESS IN QUITE SOME TIME.
PEOPLE FIND IT ENDLESSLY BORING. I'M THE KEEPER OF A GHOST TOWN, BASICALLY.
AFTER MY BOSSES PAID HANDSOMELY FOR TIJOUX'S ORIGINAL INHABITANTS TO...WELL... FUCK OFF OUT OF HERE, THEY LEFT ME HERE ALONE TO WATCH THE SHOP.
SO...HAVE COURAGE! YOURS WILL BE THE FIRST GUIDED TOUR I'VE GIVEN IN A REAL LONG TIME!
WELL, I DON'T KNOW THIS "BES" YOU'RE TALKING ABOUT.
BUT IF YOU'RE LOOKING FOR ANCIENT RELICS, THEY'RE ALL HERE IN THE MUSEUM.
?

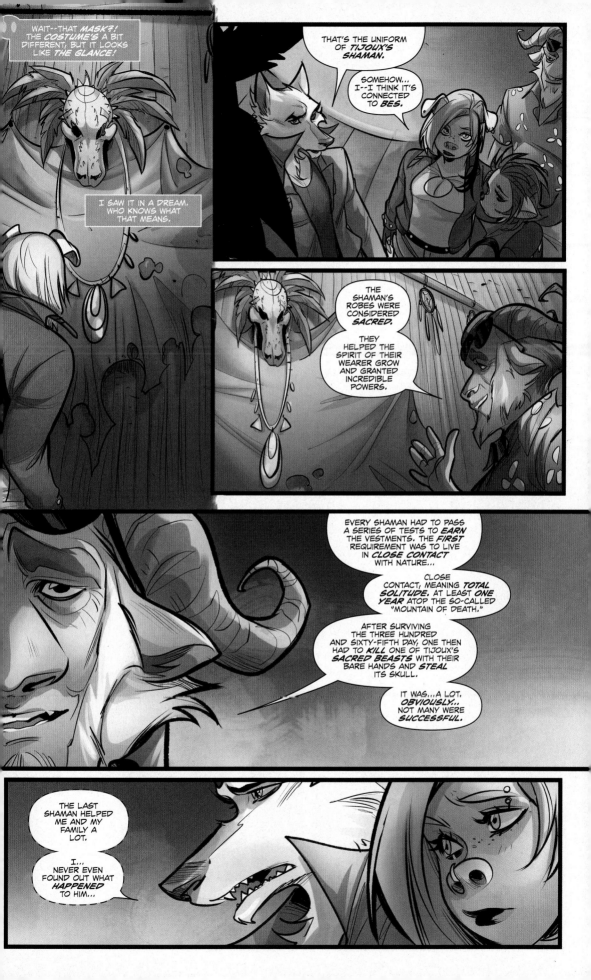

WAIT--THAT *MASK*! THE *COSTUME'S* A BIT DIFFERENT, BUT IT LOOKS LIKE *THE GLANCE*!

I SAW IT IN A DREAM. WHO KNOWS WHAT THAT MEANS.

THAT'S THE UNIFORM OF *TIJOUX'S SHAMAN.*

SOMEHOW... I--I THINK IT'S CONNECTED TO *BES.*

THE SHAMAN'S ROBES WERE CONSIDERED *SACRED.*

THEY HELPED THE SPIRIT OF THEIR WEARER GROW AND GRANTED INCREDIBLE POWERS.

EVERY SHAMAN HAD TO PASS A SERIES OF TESTS TO *EARN* THE VESTMENTS. THE *FIRST* REQUIREMENT WAS TO LIVE IN *CLOSE CONTACT* WITH NATURE...

CLOSE CONTACT, MEANING *TOTAL SOLITUDE.* AT LEAST *ONE YEAR* ATOP THE SO-CALLED "MOUNTAIN OF DEATH."

AFTER SURVIVING THE THREE HUNDRED AND SIXTY-FIFTH DAY, ONE THEN HAD TO *KILL* ONE OF TIJOUX'S *SACRED BEASTS* WITH THEIR BARE HANDS AND *STEAL* ITS SKULL.

IT WAS...A LOT. *OBVIOUSLY...* NOT MANY WERE *SUCCESSFUL.*

THE LAST SHAMAN HELPED ME AND MY FAMILY A LOT.

I.... NEVER EVEN FOUND OUT WHAT *HAPPENED* TO HIM...

DO YOU KNOW MORE ABOUT THE LAST SHAMAN, KIRK?
NOT MUCH. HE WAS OLD... FIGURED HE MUST'VE DIED YEARS AGO.
D-DEAD?
KHAL...
BUT--BUT I CAN SHOW YOU SOMETHING HE OWNED!
THIS WAS THE LAST SHAMAN'S SACRED DAGGER!
EVERY SHAMAN WAS TAUGHT THE RITUAL TO FORGE METAL, AND EVERY ONE OF THEM CREATED THEIR OWN SACRED DAGGER.
I CAN LET YOU LOOK A BIT CLOSER, IF YOU WANT.
REALLY?
SURE! NOT LIKE THERE'S ANYBODY AROUND TO FIRE ME, RIGHT?
IT'S...IT'S BEAUTIFUL...
HEY! TALL, PALE AND WOLFY!
AREN'T YOU JUST A LITTLE BIT CURIOUS?
OF COURSE! I MEAN, SURE I AM...JUST A LITTLE RATTLED, IS ALL.
TOTALLY NORMAL, KID. HERE, TAKE A CLOSER LOOK...

AND DIE, ALBINO SCUM!
!
ZROCK
WHAT?! YOU BASTARD!
YOU THINK YOU'RE A MATCH FOR ONE OF THE GREATEST HUNTERS IN THE HISTORY OF TIJOUX, YOU...GIRL?!
THUMP
YOU THOUGHT I WAS JUST A DUMB STRANGER...
BUT I RECOGNIZED YOU IMMEDIATELY. YOU AND YOUR FRIEND, BES!
SAVE THE EFFORT, WOLF! YOU'RE WEAK AS A CHILD, NOW! THIS IS NO SIMPLE DAGGER!
IT WAS SPECIFICALLY CREATED TO REACT TO YOUR MURDERER'S BLOOD!
I'M NOT A MURDERER!
SURE YOU ARE, KID! MURDER IS IN YOUR NATURE, AND YOUR KIND...
...WILL NEVER BE UNNATURAL!

HOW'S THIS FOR UNNATURAL, ASSHOLE?!
THROK
YOU--YOU SAVED ME, LES! DIDN'T YOU? OR WAS IT...
I COULDN'T LET HIM KILL YOU, KHAL.
AND YEAH, IT WAS ME.
THE ALBINO CAN'T ALWAYS CONTROL MY BODY, EVEN IF HE WISHES HE COULD.
SINCE WE'VE GOTTEN HERE, FOR SOME REASON, I'VE FELT BETTER... MORE IN CONTROL.
IT FEELS STRANGE AFTER ALL THIS TIME, ALMOST LIKE... I'VE BEEN REBORN.
THIS PLACE IS SPECIAL.
THERE ARE... MEMORIES. NOT MINE.
BES'S. I FEEL THEM, FEEL HER... INSIDE ME SOMEHOW.
I NEED TO FOLLOW THEM.

THIS PLACE, THESE OBJECTS...THANKS TO THESE MEMORIES RESURFACING, THEY'LL POINT ME TOWARDS BES.
I'LL FIND HER ANCIENT BODY, MY ANCIENT BODY... AND BE HER AGAIN.
THEN I'LL FINALLY DEFEAT THE ALBINO... FOREVER.
YOU'LL DIE, BES... YOU KNOW THAT?
YES, I DO.
AND I KNOW MY BLOOD WILL BE CURSED.
I KNOW MY LINEAGE WILL BE DAMNED.
BUT I BEG YOU, SHAMAN...
FULFILL MY LAST WISH.
WHEN I DIE, GET RID OF MY BODY...DON'T LET IT BECOME A RELIC.
LET ME GO BACK TO NATURE.
GIVE MY FLESH TO THE RIVER.

THEY'RE GONE.
BES'S REMAINS! GONE!
WHAT?
I SAW IT! SHE HAD HER BODY DESTROYED FOREVER!
THIS WAS USELESS! THERE'S NOTHING TO FIND!
WAIT, LESLIE!
YOU SEE, BRIDE? THIS IS WHAT YOU DESERVE! IT'S HOPELESS TO REJECT ME!
BUT I CAN FEEL IT NOW...YOU CAN'T HIDE YOUR FEELINGS!
YOUR HEART BURSTS WITH RAGE! NOW IS THE TIME...JOIN WITH ME!
NO!
THEY SHOULD HAVE JUST KILLED ME. IT WAS LUNACY TO HANG THEIR HOPES ON BES'S RESURRECTION.
AND IT WOULD HAVE SAVED ME THIS SUFFERING.
NO, WOMAN! DON'T DO IT! DO NOT JUMP!
CAROL SHOWED ME THE TRUTH...
THIS IS THE ONLY CHOICE. I WON'T LET YOU CONTROL ME, YOU BASTARD.

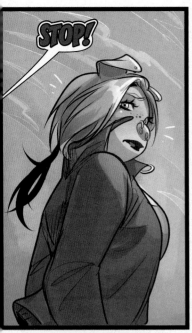

STOP!

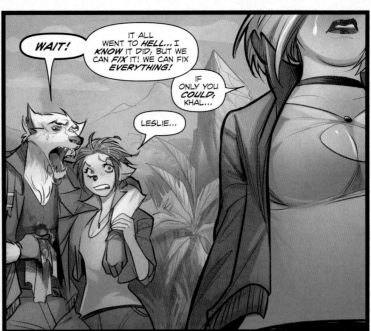

WAIT!

IT ALL WENT TO *HELL*... I *KNOW* IT DID, BUT WE CAN *FIX* IT! WE CAN FIX *EVERYTHING!*

IF ONLY YOU *COULD,* KHAL...

LESLIE...

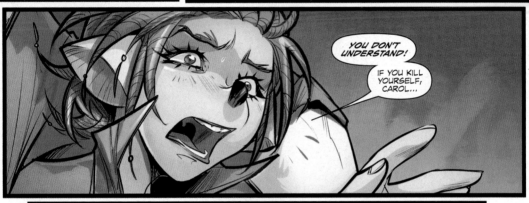

YOU DON'T UNDERSTAND!

IF YOU KILL YOURSELF, CAROL...

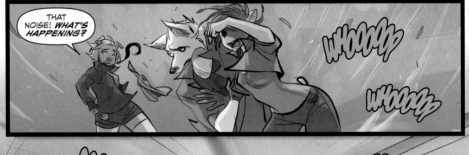

THAT NOISE! *WHAT'S* HAPPENING?

WHOOOOP

WHOOOOP

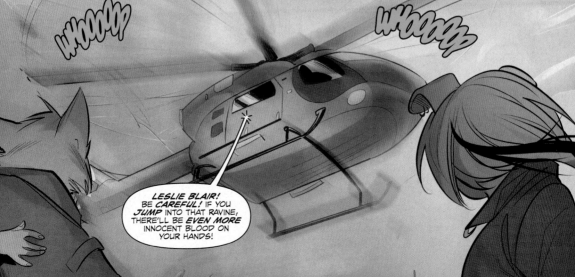

WHOOOOP

WHOOOOP

LESLIE BLAIR! BE *CAREFUL!* IF YOU *JUMP* INTO THAT RAVINE, THERE'LL BE *EVEN MORE* INNOCENT BLOOD ON YOUR HANDS!

I'VE BEEN WATCHING. DRONES ARE A WONDER THESE DAYS.
I KNOW YOUR WOLF FRIEND'S BEEN STABBED WITH A SACRED DAGGER. I KNOW THAT BES'S BODY ISN'T HERE.
THAT'S BAD... VERY BAD. THE GLANCE HAD PLANS FOR THOSE REMAINS. BUT DON'T WORRY, LESLIE...
YOUR BODY WILL MORE THAN SATISFY THE GLANCE. YOU CAN THANK YOUR FRIEND SAYA FOR THAT.
SAYA... WHAT?
I DIDN'T HAVE A CHOICE!
SHE'S JUST SOME STUPID PIG...
THEY WERE GOING TO KILL CAROL! I COULDN'T LET THEM!
"STUPID PIG"?
HOW COULD YOU DO THIS, SAYA? AFTER EVERYTHING WE'VE BEEN THROUGH?
BUT IT--IT WASN'T SUPPOSED TO END LIKE THIS.
WHO'S STUPID NOW? HOW ELSE COULD IT END?
WE'RE ALL EXPENDABLE, EVEN CAROL...
RUN, LESLIE!

EXPENDABLE? WHAT ABOUT HER, KHAL?
HELLO? ANYONE? I'M--I'M SCARED...
MY SISTER?! YOU FUCK! I--I'LL KILL YOU!
OUR SLAUGHTERHOUSE HAS A SPECIAL SECTION FOR KIDS... DID YOU KNOW THAT?
NO...NO! DON'T HURT HER!
YOU KNOW WHAT YOU MUST DO, BRIDE. I CAN SAVE YOUR FRIEND...
JUST LET ME GO FREE.
FREE...
I THINK... YOU WERE RIGHT, KHAL.
I DON'T HAVE TO BE AFRAID. I'M NOT AFRAID.
I DON'T HAVE TO WATCH AS GOOD PEOPLE LIKE YOU SUFFER.
THE ALBINO FEEDS ON MY WEAKNESS, GAINS STRENGTH FROM MY ANGER.
BUT I AM DONE BEING HIS PAWN.
YOU WANT TO MERGE, ALBINO?
OKAY, BUT LET'S GET ONE THING STRAIGHT. FROM NOW ON...

I'M IN CHARGE!
DON'T SHOOT, IDIOTS! THE GLANCE WANTS HER ALIVE!
JONES, SIR! SHE'S--
SHE'S WHAT? ALL SHE DID IS MOVE HER HAND, YOU PUSSIES!
SHE'S NOT EVEN ARMED!
?
SPLOOOTCH
KRAOOK
PLOOOT
YOU'RE RIGHT, JONES. MOVING A HAND MEANS NOTHING.
THE ALBINO DOESN'T NEED TO DO THAT. HE CAN DECREE LIFE OR DEATH WITH HIS SOLE WILL.
THAT'S WHAT YOU WANTED, RIGHT?

WHAT I WANT TO KNOW IS...
WHAT DOES THE REPRODUCTION PROGRAM WANT TO DO WITH THAT POWER?
...LES... LIE?
BAN-- fssh
TOO LATE FOR THAT, JONES.
THAT GUN WON'T HELP YOU. NOW...
TALK!
I'M NOT TELLING YOU A DAMN THING.
GO TO THE SLAUGHTERHOUSE! ASK THE GLANCE YOURSELF!
I PLAN TO, AND I PROMISE... THE GLANCE WILL BE THE FIRST TO DIE.
"YOU REALLY ARE A STUPID PIG. YOU CAN'T KILL THE GLANCE."
"IF YOU THINK I'M GOING TO FORGIVE HIM, JONES..."
FORGIVE? PERHAPS NOT, LESLIE...
"BUT, TELL ME..."
WHAT KIND OF DAUGHTER...

"WOULD RAISE A HAND AGAINST HER OWN MOTHER?!"
YOU STUPID BITCH! YOU'RE USELESS!
YOU'LL NEVER BE ABLE TO--
SPLLLLLTCH
LET'S... LET'S GO, LESLIE.
WHAT YOU DID, WE...WE HAVE TO GO. NOW.
LESLIE...
NO, THERE'S NO "LESLIE."
ME AND MY BRIDE ARE ONE, NOW.
END OF VOLUME TWO!

EXTRA
NATURAL

#LESLIEPIG
OINK

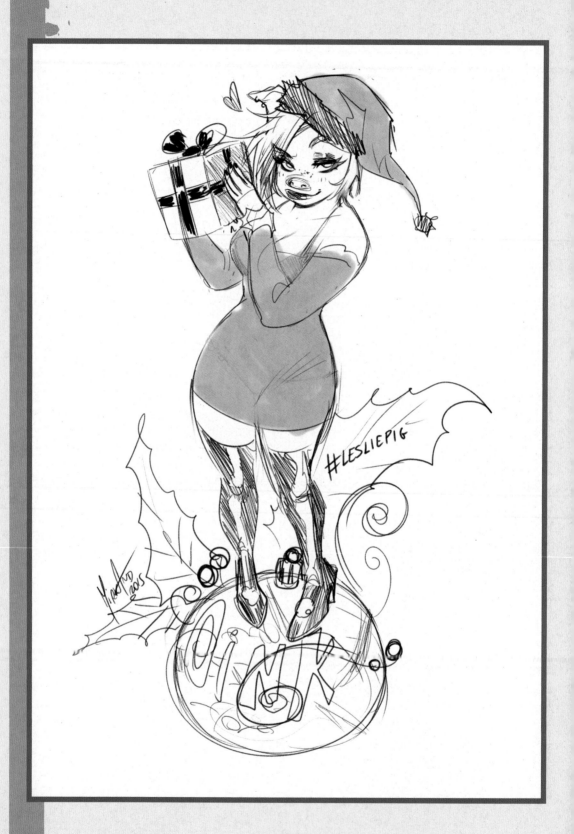

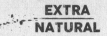
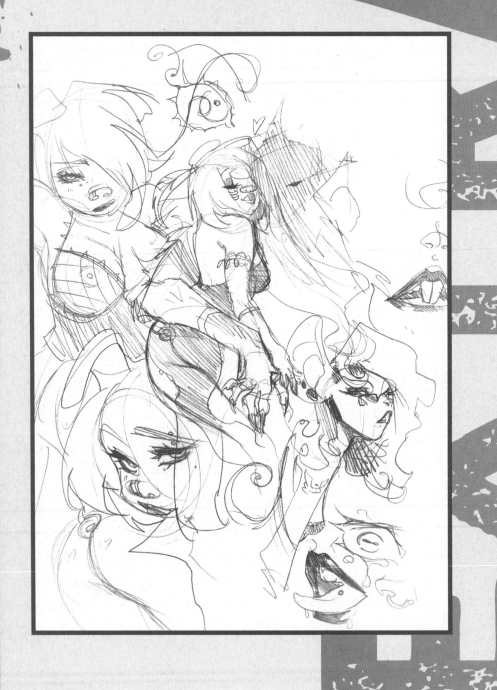

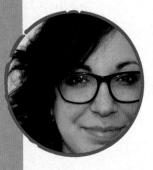

Mirka Andolfo is an Italian creator, working as an artist at DC Comics (*Harley Quinn*, *Wonder Woman*, *DC Bombshells*) and Vertigo (*Hex Wives*). She has drawn comics at Marvel, Dynamite and Aspen Comics. As a creator, *Unnatural* (published so far in Italy, Germany, France, Spain, Poland, Mexico) is her second book, after *Sacro/Profano* (published in Italy, France, Belgium, Netherlands, Spain, Germany and Serbia). You can reach Mirka on her social media channels and on her website: *mirkand.eu*

f mirkand.works   🐦 @Mirkand   📷 @mirkand89

VARIANT
COVERS

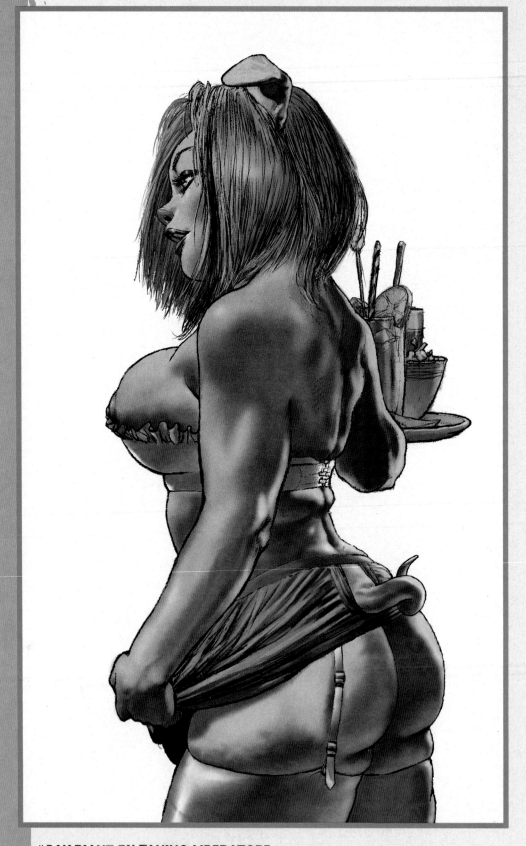

#5 VARIANT BY TANINO LIBERATORE

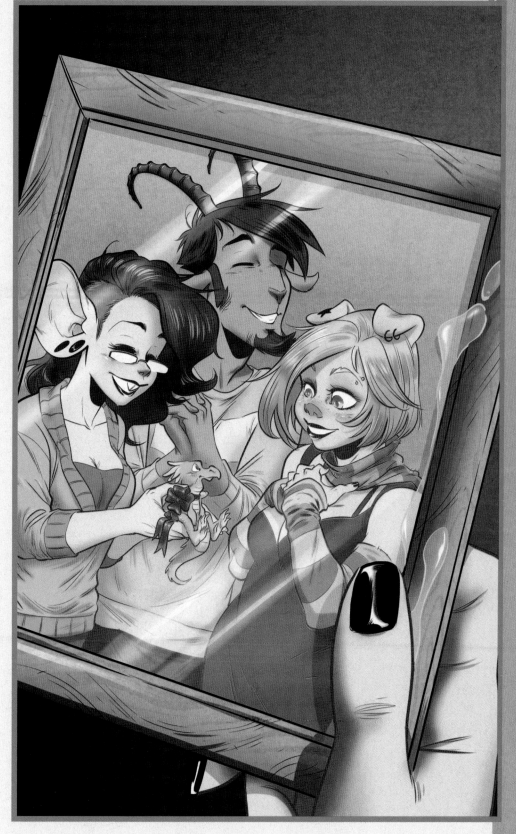

#5 HERO INITIATIVE VARIANT BY JACOPO CAMAGNI

#6 VARIANT BY BABS TARR

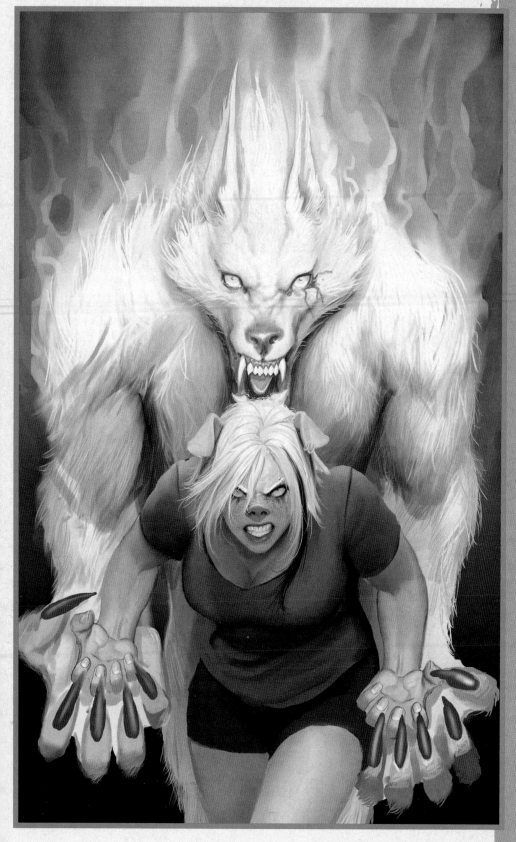

#7 VARIANT BY STJEPAN ŠEJIĆ

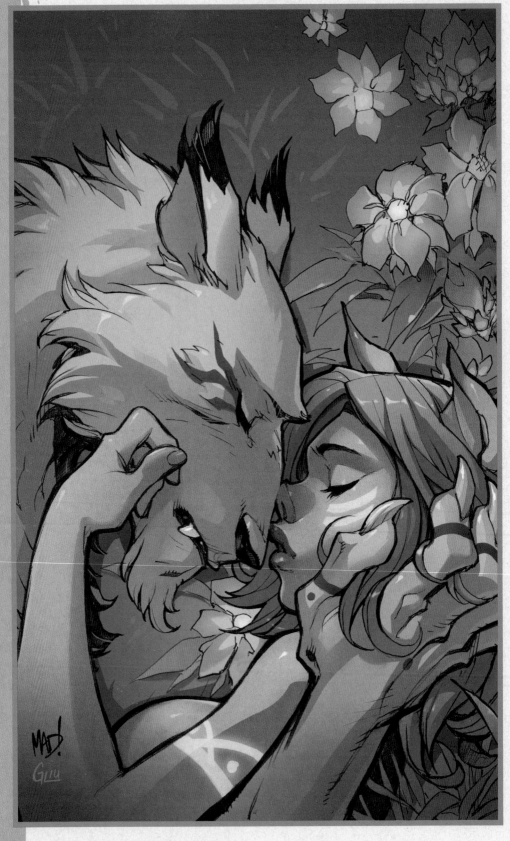

#8 VARIANT BY JOE MADUREIRA